BANG, BANG, YOU'RE DEAD!

NARINDER DHAMI

CORGI BOOKS

BANG, BANG, YOU'RE DEAD!
A CORGI BOOK 978 0 552 56043 6

Published in Great Britain by Corgi Books,
an imprint of Random House Children's Publishers UK
A Random House Group Company

This edition published 2009

9 10

**Penguin Random House is committed to a sustainable future for
our business, our readers and our planet. This book is made from
Forest Stewardship Council® certified paper.**

MIX
Paper from
responsible sources
FSC® C018179

Printed and bound in Great Britain by Clays Ltd, St Ives plc

Set in 11pt Sabon

Corgi Books are published by Random House Children's Publishers UK,
61–63 Uxbridge Road, London W5 5SA

www.**randomhousechildrens**.co.uk
www.randomhouse.co.uk

Addresses for companies within
The Random House Group Limited can be found at:
www.randomhouse.co.uk/offices.htm

THE RANDOM HOUSE GROUP Limited Reg. No. 954009

A CIP catalogue record for this book is available from the British Library.

For Robert

Dr Macdonald has asked me to tell her what happened that day.

I know she's trying to help me, but I also think she's trying to trick me.

She wants to find out exactly why I did what I did. She wants to see right inside my head, and I dislike her for that reason, amongst others.

Now that Jamie's dead and gone, I am on my own for the first time in my life.

But I think I'm strong enough to cope with that now.

So whatever Dr Macdonald thinks of me, I *will* tell her exactly what happened.

And I'll tell her the truth.

But I have a problem.

Who in the world is going to believe me?

One

The scene is normal: a family at breakfast on Monday morning before the kids go off to school.

But the people in the scene are not normal. Our mother is hurtling headlong into one of her manic phases after weeks of depression. She flits around the kitchen, unable to sit still, talking about nothing at all without stopping. Her latest idea is to keep chickens in the back garden to save on buying eggs. I don't like eggs, Jamie never eats them and Mum's allergic to feathers.

My twin brother sits opposite me. He doesn't eat anything, he doesn't speak and he doesn't look at either Mum or me. He stares morosely at the kitchen floor, lost in a world of his own. Jamie's long ago given up on Mum and the bizarre lottery of her behaviour,

3

the endless swings between highs and lows. They have no relationship with each other. Jamie and I were close once, but now that closeness is slipping away too. All he and I seem to do is argue. I can't rely on him like I used to. Some of the things he says frighten me.

I am Mia, the glue that holds this whole sinking ship together, and, believe me, we're sinking fast.

Our father isn't part of this happy scene. He left Mum before we were born and they divorced soon after. We've never seen him and we don't even know his name. Mum refuses to tell.

'We could take in lodgers,' Mum prattles on. She drags a stepladder over to the tall cupboards and energetically begins to fling pots and pans onto the worktop. 'This kitchen needs a good clean. I was thinking we could do up the attic. There's plenty of room in there.'

'Oh, God,' Jamie mutters, the first thing he's said this morning.

'It's certainly an idea, Mum,' I say in my usual placatory tone. 'We could do with the extra money.'

Jamie is here, I'm sure of it. I feel it so strongly that

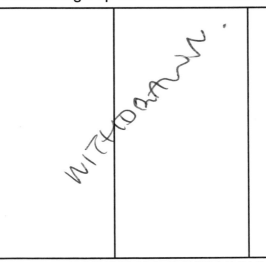

Jamie rolls his eyes and shoots me a contemptuous stare, blaming me for encouraging Mum. But I know that the lodgers, like the chickens in the back garden, will never happen. By the time Mum gets around to doing anything about it, she'll probably be depressed again and lie in bed for weeks.

She's had medication to help control the mood swings, but since Grandpa died she's stopped taking it. I can't bear to argue with her. That's another thing Jamie blames me for. He says I'm too soft. He says there must be *someone* who can help us – doctors, Social Services, *anyone*. We've tried all this before. But Mum hates doctors and hospitals and outside interference with a passion, and cries like a child if I suggest a visit to the surgery. She doesn't keep hospital appointments and hides if anyone official comes to the house.

'I'll go shopping today, then.' Mum abandons the cupboard half emptied, grabs a mop and begins swishing it vigorously around the floor. 'We'll need beds and curtains and carpets and wardrobes and—'

His face thunderous, Jamie jumps up and stalks

out of the kitchen, flinging the door open with a crash. Anxious to calm him down, I immediately get up to follow. But Mum does not even look.

I can't blame Jamie. We have no money and Mum can't hold down a job, so we live on benefits and every so often we have to sell some of Grandpa's precious treasures for pennies. That I *hate*, more than anything. But when Mum's manic, she shops. A few months ago we came home from school to find a brand-new black Mercedes convertible parked on the drive. It went straight back to the dealer and Mum sulked for days. Yesterday she was talking about getting a Harley Davidson motorbike. She doesn't have a driving licence.

Credit-card bills pile through the letter box every month, but Mum ignores them and simply applies for new cards. I don't know how she gets them. I have a nasty feeling that fraud may be involved.

When Jamie and I were three years old, we lost our home because Mum couldn't pay the rent, and that's how we ended up moving in with Grandpa. He was the only one who could do anything at all with Mum, but he died just over a year ago. I can't describe how much I loved him and how much I miss him. I won't try.

This enormous, rambling, tumbledown old house feels too big and lonely now. It's a strange house, cold and overheated at the same time, with redbrick towers and turrets and gloomy stained-glass windows and doors, like a haunted church.

The kids in our street call us the Addams Family. That might be because of the house, or it could be because they think we're strange. They don't speak to us. They just shout names at us sometimes.

'Got to go, Mum.' I pause in the doorway. 'See you later.'

Mum drops the mop in the middle of the floor and rushes over to give me an enormous hug. She is so beautiful, tall and slender with the most amazing long black curls. You'd never know to look at her that she is ill.

'Have a lovely day, sweetheart!' Mum sings to the tune of the song playing on the radio. 'And don't worry about me, I'll be fine.'

I nod, although I *will* worry and she knows that I

will. But that doesn't stop her from being hair-raisingly reckless in everything she does when the mania overtakes her again.

Knowing that Jamie will be hovering accusingly in the hall, blaming me, I try desperately to salvage something from the situation.

'About the lodger, Mum. It's a good idea, but maybe you'd better wait until we've cleared out the attic before you buy any furniture—'

Mum's face changes. 'Why?' she snaps. Her whole stance is instantly angry and aggressive, and I wilt at the challenging expression in her eyes.

'Well . . .' I stumble, wishing I'd just let it go, like I do ninety-nine times out of a hundred. Caught between trying to please Mum and trying to placate Jamie, I end up pleasing no one. 'We're a bit short of money at the moment—'

Furiously Mum kicks out at the mop. It hurtles across the floor towards me and I jump backwards to avoid being struck.

'I have money!' Mum shouts. She is cold and hard and raging. 'I have three new credit cards!'

'I just thought maybe we could clear some space first,' I mutter, edging over to the door. I should have followed my survival instincts and said nothing. Why do I always make the wrong decision on those rare occasions when I make a decision at all?

'Mia, keep your nose out of my business!' Mum shrieks like a wild banshee. I've seen this unreasonable, ranting anger before and it doesn't last, but it always scares me. 'You're just a kid, so don't meddle in things that don't concern you! The money is *my* responsibility!'

'Shut *up*, Mum!' Jamie has returned to stand in the doorway beside me. He looks no less angry and aggressive than Mum herself. They're more alike than either of them realize. 'You're *pathetic*, do you know that? You don't give a toss about anyone but yourself—'

Mum grabs a plate and hurls it wildly at us. I duck, but Jamie does not move. The plate misses us and smashes into pieces as it hits the floor.

'Stop it,' Mum moans, clutching at her hair. 'I'm sick of you going on at me! Go away! Get out of my face and leave me alone!'

'It's all right, Mum,' I say quickly. 'It's OK. Get whatever you like.'

I am desperate to leave now, but Jamie still stands there, furious and frustrated.

I grab his arm and drag him out into the hallway. There he pulls himself away from me and sits on the bottom stair, burying his head in his hands. I glance back into the kitchen and see that Mum is still shaking with rage. Leaving the mop on the floor, she sits down at the kitchen table, lifting her knees and curling herself into a tight ball. I close the door quietly.

It's her illness, I tell myself, as I always do. *She can't help it*.

But the mantra is losing its power after years of repetition. After the shattering events of last week, I know we can no longer go on like this. But the alternative fills me with cold dread.

Jamie is still angry and he's restless. As he sits, he taps his feet impatiently on the diamond-patterned floor of the hallway. The black and white Victorian tiles badly need polishing and at least six of them are cracked. There are pieces of wood nailed over the missing rectangles of stained glass in the front door. The house is going downhill too since Grandpa died.

'Why do you do it, Mia?' Jamie demands. His dark eyes scald me, and I can sense the tension in him, like a cornered animal ready to fight to the death. 'Why do you give in to her?'

'Don't start,' I sigh.

'You know this can't go on,' Jamie mutters, mirroring my own thought of a moment ago.

'Well, help me then!' I cry in frustration. 'Tell me what to do!'

Jamie shakes his head. 'When will you learn, Mia?' he says wearily. 'I can't do this on my own and *you* won't stand up to Mum, so things are spinning out of control. You've *got* to get tough. You can't rely on me for ever.' He pauses, looks away from me, and I tense, guessing what is coming next. 'What would you do if – well, if I wasn't around any more?'

My insides freeze with fear. He has said something like this before, several times, and I still have no idea

11

what he really means. I don't ask. I *won't* ask. I'm too frightened.

'Don't be stupid,' I say with a nervous laugh. 'I wish you wouldn't say stuff like that. You're not going anywhere.'

Jamie looks away and does not answer. Terror closes up my throat and I can hardly speak. What's going on inside his head? Once, I would have known. Now my own brother is a deep, dark and, I think, dangerous mystery.

'You wouldn't . . . leave me to cope on my own?' I croak.

Jamie gives me an odd look. 'Everything's all wrong,' he says in a low voice, more intense and frightening than if he'd shouted the words aloud. 'And I'm tired of trying to make it right.'

Jamie stands and trudges up the stairs, grinding misery in every step he takes. I go after him, but he stops and looks back towards me at the turn of the stair.

'You remember what I said to you last week, Mia?' he murmurs quietly. 'I told you, I warned you. If Mum won't help herself, then we have to force her to realize what her illness is doing to us.'

'Push her to the edge, you said,' I whisper. 'Make her sit up and take notice.'

I am shaking. This is the moment I knew was coming, and I'm terrified beyond belief. 'You said we have to make her see that she can't go on like this, and neither can we.'

Jamie nods. His dark eyes are burning through me. 'It's time,' he says.

My knees buckle at the grim determination in his voice. 'But – what are you going to do?' I gasp. 'Jamie? *What?*'

Jamie stares down at me. His expression is closed and unreadable, but there is a hint of sadness in his eyes.

'I can't tell you, Mia,' he says simply, and then he vanishes upstairs.

I am left sick with anxiety.

I know Jamie's right. This can't go on. But I'm too weak and too pathetic to do anything about it. I'm a quiet little mouse who likes to fade into the background and stay there. Jamie and I look very much alike – anyone would guess that we're twins – but I'm a pale imitation of him, a shadow image. We both have dark hair, but Jamie's is shiny and glossy and mine is lank and drab. My brown eyes, the exact shade and shape of Jamie's, are as dull as his are alive. Jamie is tall and athletic while I'm the same size as him, but too bony with it. There's nothing special about me in any way whatsoever. Jamie is five minutes younger than I am, but he not only got the good looks, he also got all the spirit and the personality and the drive. He's not afraid of anything. Me, I'm not the type to make a fuss or stand up for myself. I take whatever's handed out to me.

Last week, stupid fool that I am, I started to think that maybe I *wasn't* so ordinary. It didn't last long, of course. I was so thrilled to win the essay competition, but now the whole thing has turned into a disaster. How could I not have known? Nothing good ever happens to me without something bad following close behind.

The essay was all Ms Kennedy's fault.

Ms Kennedy has been my favourite teacher ever since I started at Hollyfield School. She and I discuss novels all the time – *really* discuss them. We debate, and we even argue occasionally. Ms Kennedy lends me books and praises my stories, and she says I should think about a career as a writer. Me, Mia the mouse, a writer!

Ms Kennedy actually treats me seriously, as if I'm worthy of respect. Not many people do that. But it was Ms Kennedy who persuaded me to enter that essay competition, and I've been teased relentlessly about it ever since. Now I almost hate her. Well, I would if I could summon up the energy . . .

I pick up my school bag and into it I slip the copy of *Pride and Prejudice* that Ms Kennedy lent me. It's comfort reading, a world where everything is governed by good manners and rules of behaviour. It sounds heavenly.

I leave to get the bus to school. Jamie is nowhere to be seen, but that's nothing unusual these days. We always used to travel together but now he disappears and turns up at school whenever. I never see him on the way, and I dare not enquire where he goes or whom he sees or what he's been doing. There is so much more to Jamie than meets the eye, and I'm too scared to ask him what I long to know.

Especially today.

I wish I had some idea what he was planning.

I can't tell you, Mia.

Does that mean Jamie doesn't yet know what he's going to do, or does he mean that it's too horrific to tell me? I hope desperately that it's the former option.

'How's your mum today, Mia?'

I am near the school gates when I hear the inevitable shout. I don't turn to look because I already know who it is. Kat Randall and her gang of witch-faced cronies, whose sole aim, since last week, is to make my school life a misery.

I don't reply to the question because it's the same every morning. For the first three years at Hollyfield, no one knew about Mum except some of the teachers and Bree, my best friend. Last week Kat Randall found out about her. I still go hot and cold with humiliation when I think about what happened.

Kat Randall clumps over to me in designer trainers with thick rubber soles. Her school tie has the thickest knot and shortest length it can possibly have, and her skirt is twenty centimetres above her fat knees. She wears her dirty blonde hair gelled straight back, with two long curls stuck to her cheeks, one on each side. Kat is hard in every sense of the word. She had a fist fight with her ex-boyfriend, Lee Curtis, in the playground last week. And believe me, Lee Curtis – who has just been suspended for dealing weed at school – is bigger and harder and even more terrifying than Kat herself. But Kat seems to fear nothing and no one. Her quest in life is to seek out and destroy the vulnerable. Sadly, I am her latest target.

'Didn't you hear me, Jackson?' Kat enquires with a mock-friendly smile. 'I said, how's your mum?'

I long to keep quiet and defy her, but I'm not brave enough now she is standing right in front of me.

'She's fine,' I mumble. I hardly understand Mum's illness myself, and Jamie doesn't even try, so how can I expect a group of hatchet-faced, dead-eyed girls with all the sense and intelligence of an amoeba to have any kind of sympathy?

'Still raving mad?' Kat asks gleefully, and her minions standing around us chortle at her wit. Kat Randall and her friends are in the lowest sets for every subject, and they are not intelligent. But they're very skilled in the subtleties of mental torture.

I wonder what Kat would do if I lunged forward, grabbed each ridiculous curl and pulled very hard.

'She's not mad, she's ill,' I mutter, trying to edge my way past them. 'I told you.'

Kat thrusts her face very close to mine. She's been eating salt and vinegar crisps for breakfast.

'And I told *you*, she's *mad*,' she spits. With one quick movement, so quick I don't even have time to gasp, she grabs my school tie and tightens it, almost choking me. I stagger back, frantically pulling to loosen it, and Kat smiles with complete satisfaction as she hangs onto it so I'm like a dog on a lead.

'All alone again, I see?' she remarks, making an elaborate pantomime of looking over her shoulder. 'So, are you going to run and tell tales to Ms Kennedy?

18

We all know how much you *luuurve* her, you lezzer.'

And Kat laughs and releases my tie and strolls away, glowing visibly with the knowledge of her power over me. Her cronies follow, twittering with admiration.

Shaking, I loosen my tie and take a gulp of air. I can't help feeling bitter. Jamie has kept well out of this situation with Kat Randall so far. At one time he would have rushed to defend me in some way, but not any longer.

So far it's only been the verbal stuff. I can put up with that. This is the first time Kat's ever actually touched me. That probably means we're escalating towards actual violence, and the thought leaves me strangely unmoved.

'You're so stupid, Mia. How long are you going to let them get away with this?'

I spin round. Jamie's come up silently behind me and he's staring at me with that same frightening, burning intensity. I guess he watched what was going on from a distance, but made no move to help me.

I shrug helplessly. 'What can I do?'

'*Mia!*'

19

Jamie's agonized cry of sheer frustration makes me squirm. I *know* I'm stupid and weak, but it just feels like I have no energy left any more, for *anything*. It seems like everything that was uniquely me, uniquely Mia, has drained away over the years of struggle and left me an empty shell.

'You could help—' I begin.

'You have to learn to stand up for *yourself*!' Jamie interrupts me. He sounds so fierce, almost evangelical. 'Do you really think you're worth so little, Mia? Christ, is this how you're going to live your life? Letting everyone walk all over you?'

I am silent. Sadly, that's exactly what I can see happening to me now and for ever.

'I've had enough.' Jamie's always restless, but today he can't stop tapping his feet, flexing his fingers, running his hands again and again through his long dark hair. His face is pure dead white. I get the fearful, maybe fanciful, notion that he has reached some sort of breaking point. That there is a line in the sand and he has crossed it and now there is no going back. 'I'm sick of it all.'

He looks not at me, but through me, something indefinable in his eyes. Recklessness? Whatever it is, it reminds me of Mum and I tremble.

'I'm going to make everyone sit up and take notice, including Mum,' he says softly. 'It's payback time.'

Before I can speak, Jamie marches away and there is a steely purpose in his manner. I run after him as he weaves his way through the groups of pupils in the playground, but he is quickly out of sight. I wonder if I should be worried. I think I know something about what Jamie is capable of from things that have happened in the past, but I push the fear away because I don't *want* to acknowledge it. That's my weakness again.

'Hey, Mia!'

My best friend Bree is waving at me from the other side of the playground. Cheerful, bouncy, blonde Bree with her smooth pink and white complexion. She should be in a TV ad for something healthy and wholesome like milk or Swiss cheese. We've been friends since primary school. Bree's always been prettier and more popular than me, but when we were in Year Four, her mother had severe depression and Bree latched onto me for support. Her mum recovered eventually, but Bree didn't drop me. She's loyal and funny and kind. She talks too much, but I let her conversation wash over me a lot of the time. It's very healing, like lying in a warm, scented bath, because it's so *normal*.

'So, Daniel calls me last night . . .' Bree begins as soon as I join her.

I listen as she recounts her conversation with her boyfriend Daniel in mind-numbingly minute detail. Daniel is trying to persuade Bree to sleep with him, and Bree isn't sure she wants to. I think how wonderful it would be if my only problem was trying to decide whether to sleep with a good-looking (if slightly arrogant) boy or not. I've never had a boyfriend, unless you count Callum Carter, who used to chase me around the playground at primary school and kiss me. But I suppose someone who's desperate might ask me out eventually. I can't imagine *ever* introducing a boyfriend to Mum, though. If she's in a manic phase, she'd probably flirt with him and try to sit on his lap. If she's depressed, she might easily burst into tears in front of him. It hardly seems worth the embarrassment.

'And then he said if I *really* loved him, I'd *want* to do it,' Bree goes on.

'That old line?' I say, raising my eyebrows. 'I would have thought Daniel could come up with something a bit more original than *that*.'

Bree giggles.

No, it's not the sex that would bother me, but I don't like the thought of sleeping with someone else. Someone who could watch me while I was sleeping. I can't imagine trusting anyone enough to let that happen.

Now I *know* you think I'm seriously strange.

The bell rings and we all shuffle reluctantly towards the school entrance.

From this point, things happen fast.

Bree and I go to our classroom on the second floor where the usual morning riot is taking place. Jamie is not there. I'm surprised, and also worried.

'Where's Jamie today, Mia?' someone calls across the classroom above the cacophony of gossip and giggles.

I ignore whoever it is, not even turning round. I know they're only being nasty, teasing me because they know how much my brother means to me now. But I can't talk about Jamie right at this moment. I don't know why, but a sense of doom, black and impenetrable, is sweeping over me, chilling my bones.

Bree glances at me and opens her mouth. I suspect she's going to ask me about Jamie too, and I don't want to hear it. Abruptly I turn away and pretend to be intent on searching for something in my bag.

'Sit down and get your books out and shut up, Nine A!' yells our form tutor, Ms Powell, arriving with the register.

Bree is now talking to Lee Hung, who sits on the other side of her. I rest my head against the window next to our table and wonder, with immense weariness, how long it will be before Kat Randall gets tired of tormenting me and searches for a fresh victim. I wish I could do something, anything, to get her off my back. But I can't because I'm a coward, pure and simple . . .

Then, as I stare into the playground below me, I see Jamie. His head is down and his shoulders are hunched, but there is a grim purpose in his walk. He's not coming towards our part of the school. He's heading over to the other side, in the direction of the annexe. Hollyfield is quite old, built in the seventies, and extra bits have been added onto the main building over the last twenty years or so. The two-storey annexe is connected to the school by a long glass corridor. The annexe is where Class 9D have their form room on the first floor. Kat Randall and her friends are in Class 9D.

Jamie, what are you doing? I ask silently. *Speak to me.*

Once my brother and I had a kind of telepathy between us, as twins often do. It was rather hit-and-miss, and as elusive, fleeting and fragile as a butterfly's wing. But since Grandpa died we seem to have lost this too, most of the time. Jamie has become skilled at shutting me out and now, unsurprisingly, he does not answer me.

Why is he going to the annexe?

Something terrible is about to happen.

I know it.

I stumble to my feet. People are still milling around

the room, Bree is deep in conversation with Lee Hung, and Ms Powell is coping with lost dinner money and forgotten homework crises. I slip out of the classroom, unnoticed.

The corridors are deserted because no one is allowed out of their form rooms again until the bell for morning lessons. *I'm breaking a school rule.* The very thought of such a thing makes me feel sick. Mia Jackson doesn't break the rules. She's too much of a scaredy-cat. I'm shaking all over but it's not just because I'm doing something I'm not supposed to.

I am terrified, but I don't know why.

I head towards the nearest set of stairs, but I hear hurrying footsteps coming towards me. Panicking, I scurry out of sight behind a bookcase before whoever it is rounds the corner. Then I wait there for what seems like hours but is probably no more than five minutes. I hear more footsteps, then, a little later, muffled, urgent voices. More footsteps, running this time.

I am paralysed behind my bookcase with the fear of discovery. I don't even know why I came out of the classroom. Jamie may have had a perfectly acceptable reason for going to the annexe, nothing to do with Kat Randall at all. In fact, he might even be on his way back to our classroom right now . . .

Suddenly the fire alarm bursts into life right above my head, shrill, insistent and unnerving.

With a shocked gasp, I leap out from behind the bookcase with my hands over my ears. But it doesn't matter that I'm out in the open now because a second later doors are flung wide, and pupils and teachers pour out of the classrooms and head towards the emergency exits like rivers streaming towards the sea.

I melt anonymously into the crowd. I can hear screaming behind me, and some of the teachers look dead white and very frightened. A real fire, then? My heart skips a beat. *Jamie?*

'Mia!' Someone grabs my arm as the stream of human beings flows past our classroom. I turn and look into Bree's petrified face.

'Where the *hell* have you been, Mia?' she shrieks hysterically, digging her nails painfully into my arm. 'We *have* to get out of here!'

'There's a fire, then?' I ask, dreading the answer,

wondering if it has been started deliberately . . .

Bree shakes her head. 'Worse,' she gasps. She is almost hyperventilating and is trembling violently from head to toe. 'There's a rumour that someone is in school with a gun.'

Two

Monday 10 March, 8.56 a.m.

Time seems to stand still.

'A *gun*?' I repeat.

I have to force my lips to form those two simple words.

Bree nods abruptly, wrapping her arms around herself and rocking to and fro. A group of Year Eight girls rush past us, white-faced, shrieking, and nearly bowl Bree over.

'Now can we *please* get out of here?' Bree screams.

She turns and makes to flee with everyone else towards the fire escape, but I catch her arm. I twist her round to face me, against the flow of the crowd.

'Who is it?' I yell. The sound of my heartbeat booms in my ears. 'Who's got a gun? Who is it, Bree? *Tell me!*'

As I yell, I grip Bree by both arms. But it takes me a moment to realize I'm shaking her so hard that her eyes are rolling in her head.

'For God's sake, Mia!' Bree drags herself from my grasp. Tears are pouring down her cheeks. 'I just told you that there might be a *gunman* in here! Haven't you seen what happened in those schools in America? Get out of my way!'

She shoves me aside and runs, along with everyone else. I'm now so petrified myself, I can hardly breathe, but I chase after her, desperate for answers.

'Sorry,' I gasp as I run beside her. I can't bring myself to say anything about Jamie or even mention his name, but inside my head I see him striding towards the annexe, stern and purposeful. 'Bree, I'm *sorry*! But is it really true? It *can't* be!'

'Well, take a look around you,' Bree snaps, not glancing at me, her eyes fixed unblinkingly on the emergency exit directly ahead of us. The doors are open and outside, down in the playground, I can see teachers frantically urging hysterical, screaming pupils to run away from the school and across to the car park.

'Seems pretty convincing, wouldn't you say?'

'But *who* is it?' I am now trembling and shaking as violently as Bree herself. '*Who?* Is it . . . someone we know?'

What I think *can't* be possible.

There are *so many* reasons why it can't be possible.

And yet . . .

'Oh, hell, Mia,' Bree sobs as she jostles and pushes to get to the exit more quickly. 'I don't bloody know *anything*, all right? There are texts and phone calls flying around the whole school, and who knows how many of them are true? Someone said he's in the annexe. Someone else said he's wearing a mask. It might be a pupil but no one knows for *sure*.'

'Someone must know,' I scream. My face feels wet, so I must be crying too.

I can't bring myself to say any more. I am frantic with fear. And yet I'm really angry and full of pent-up frustration too. I want to know what's going on and no one's telling me anything. I am so *furious*, I feel like I could punch someone. If Kat Randall was in front of me now, I *would* punch her. But she isn't here. She's in the annexe.

With Jamie?

It seems utterly unbelievable that the gunman is Jamie. But on the other hand, I remember things that have happened in the past. Dark, mysterious things with Jamie at the heart of them.

Bree does not say anything more either. She puts on a final, magnificent burst of speed and hurtles out through the open doors onto the fire escape.

She probably assumes I'll follow her, but I don't. Instead, I flatten myself against the wall to avoid the relentless flow of bodies and begin to edge away from the open doors and back down the corridor.

No one notices me, not even the teachers. The entire corridor is crammed with heaving, pushing, shoving, screaming bodies. One single mass of pure blind fear, everyone alike, teachers and pupils. No one cares about looking cool when they might be staring death in the face.

As I inch my way along the corridor wall past our open classroom door, my mind spins so much that I actually feel seasick. Jamie's voice sings in my ears above the screams.

I've had enough.

I'm going to make everyone sit up and take notice, including Mum.

It's payback time.

What did he mean? I *have* to find out exactly what is happening. My life and maybe the lives of others too depend on it.

The waves of bodies seem endless and suddenly I am tired of fighting my way against the tide. My back bumps against the handle of a cupboard door. Fumbling behind me, I turn the handle and manage to open the door a little way so that I can slip inside.

I close the door softly, with relief. The hysterical screams and pounding footsteps are now muffled, and in the relative quiet I can at least attempt to collect my shattered thoughts. But surely someone in that huge crowd noticed me, saw me slip away? I wait with pounding heartbeat for the inevitable shout, the wrenching open of the cupboard door. But nothing happens.

My legs shaking uncontrollably, I edge my way over to the tiny window on the other side of the cupboard. I stare outside, over the window ledge.

High up, I have a very good view of the playground and car park. I can see my class, including Bree, huddled together in a state of shock, screaming and crying. Even the loudest, the most arrogant and the most badly behaved boys have their arms around each other.

Jamie is not there.

I glance to my left, at the annexe. Pupils are still pushing and shoving their way out of the side doors where teachers stand, directing them to join their year groups in the car park. I strain my eyes and squint through the bright winter sunshine, trying to catch a glimpse of Jamie.

He is not there either. Nor can I see a single pupil from Kat Randall's class, 9D, or their form tutor, Mrs Lucas.

I wait and watch until the flood of students from the annexe becomes a trickle. There is still no sign of Jamie or Kat Randall and the rest of Class 9D, including Mrs Lucas. As I watch, willing all of them to appear, I hear the wailing sirens of police cars heading towards the school.

Exhausted and trembling, I sit down on a stack of copies of *Macbeth*. I have no idea why I'm here or what I'm going to do. I don't know where Jamie is, or even if he is the person with the gun.

I must be mad to even think of it, I tell myself. *It can't be him.*

And yet, if not, why am I here? Why didn't I flee the school along with Bree and everyone else?

I bury my face in my hands as I acknowledge the earth-shattering truth: I'm here because I suspect that it *is* Jamie. His words this morning, the way he looked, the misery burning in his eyes, the tension within him that screamed he was on the edge – despite everything that common sense tells me, all of these things mean I *have* to believe it's him. And there is *no way* I can leave my twin brother to face this on his own.

I know with sickening certainty that Class 9D will still be in the annexe with him. Some of them may never even come out alive. I *cannot* have that on my conscience, even if he's gone after Kat Randall and her gang for my sake.

But I know that only a small part of this is about me and Kat Randall. This is all about Mum, and the fragmented, unbearable disorder of our life together. It must be, because this is what Jamie promised me would happen. He told me that he would force Mum, by whatever means possible, to realize what her illness and her stubborn refusal to deal with it is doing to us.

This is Jamie's final, desperate gesture to get an uncaring world to wake up and take notice. Maybe it is his last gift to me before he 'leaves' me.

Or, even more terrifying, has Jamie cracked and gone under, disappearing inside himself, so that he no longer knows exactly what he's doing?

Is it possible that Jamie has a gun?

Yes, it is perfectly possible.

You see, I know where the gun came from.

Three

Eleven years earlier

Before we moved in with Grandpa, we lived in a small, narrow flat at the top of a tower block in Birmingham. It only had one bedroom, Jamie's and mine, and Mum slept on the sofa in the living room. Looking back now, I realize that the estate was a stereotype, like something out of a Channel Four drama: run-down tower blocks looming over concrete walkways, hoodies hanging around on the corners, the odd burned-out car. The lifts didn't work and smelled of pee, and it wasn't uncommon to turn a corner and find someone slumped on the steps with a bag of glue in their hand.

Only three years old, Jamie and I didn't notice much of this. We spent a lot of time indoors because Mum hated living on the estate and this seemed to trigger her depression. She'd go to bed and stay there. Days would turn into weeks, and weeks into months. Meanwhile Jamie and I fed and washed ourselves and put ourselves to bed, after a fashion. But I don't remember ever being anxious. In those days Jamie and I were happy if we were together, and we were together all the time.

One rainy day Jamie and I were playing our favourite game in the damp, tunnel-like hallway of the flat. This involved dashing from one end of the hall to the other and jumping over the frayed holes in the carpet where the crocodiles lived. We were trying to do this as quietly as possible because Mum was asleep, and we had to keep clapping our hands over our mouths to muffle our giggles.

Suddenly there was a knock at the door. My eyes wide, I looked at Jamie in an agony of indecision.

'Who *is* it?' I whispered. We didn't get many visitors. Those who did come usually wanted money.

'I don't know,' Jamie whispered back.

We both stood there staring at the door, and Jamie put his thumb in his mouth, which he always did when he was worried.

'Shall we tell Mum?' I asked.

'Why?' Jamie replied, very reasonably. 'She won't *do* anything.'

We already knew all about Mum's illness, even though we were so very young.

'It might be the King of the Crocodiles,' I told Jamie solemnly. 'Let's creep away before he gobbles us both up for his dinner.'

We were about to tiptoe away into our bedroom when the battered flap of the letter box shot up. A pair of familiar kind, blue eyes looked in at us.

Chuckling with delight, I bowled down the hall towards the front door. 'It's Grandpa, Jamie! It's Grandpa!'

Grandpa lived just a few miles away, but he'd only been visiting for the last couple of months. He and Mum hadn't spoken for years after a huge family row. I never found out the whole story, but I think Mum had stolen money from him and Gran. Gran was dead of a heart attack by this time, and Grandpa was on his own.

'Hello, my darling,' Grandpa said to me through the letter box. He was a tall, upright, ex-military man and our letter box was quite low down so he must have either bent double or got down on his knees. 'How are you?'

'We're very well, thank you,' I replied in my best polite voice. 'Jamie bumped his head on the door yesterday, but he's all right now.'

'I'm glad to hear it,' said Grandpa, smiling at Jamie, who had run to stand next to me. 'Hello, Jamie. Now, where's your mummy?'

'Mum's in bed,' Jamie and I said together.

Even through the narrow flap of the letter box, I could see that Grandpa was frowning.

'In bed?' he repeated. 'But I thought you'd be all packed up and ready to leave by now.'

Jamie and I were too puzzled by this to reply.

'You're coming to live with me today,' Grandpa went on. 'Didn't your mum tell you? It's all arranged.'

We'd never been to Grandpa's house. He was always inviting us, but Mum hadn't felt well enough to go yet. But I suppose, even at only three years old, I must have immediately thought that it couldn't be any worse than the flat, could it? And it had one definite advantage:

Grandpa would be there.

I remember it was grey and raining outside and the flat was dark and cold. But suddenly I was filled to overflowing with hope and happiness. And Jamie's face mirrored my feelings.

'Thanks, Grandpa!' he gasped. He danced around the hall, not even bothering to jump over the crocodiles, singing, '*We're going to live with Grandpa.*'

I don't know what Grandpa said to Mum that day. But he had her up and dressed in fifteen minutes. There was a van and two removal men waiting outside for us and an hour later everything had been packed and we were gone.

Grandpa lived in a quiet, leafy suburb on the very edge of the city. The enormous house was a box of delights, an Aladdin's cave of mystery and wonder, a treasure trove of the beautiful and the ugly, the useful and the useless. Grandpa had spent a lot of his life in the army, and he and Gran had travelled all over the world. They were collectors and hoarders, and every corner of every room, every cupboard, every drawer, every chest was packed with objects. Here there would be a tall, carved wooden bird standing on one spindly leg, there a box of jewel-coloured teacups with matching saucers, nestled in blue velvet. There were stacks of dusty books and old magazines, and stuffed animals stared at us from dark corners with their glassy, unblinking eyes.

I had my own bedroom and it was vast and cavernous and stuffed with antiques from the four corners of the globe. Even the cover on my bed was oriental, a deep turquoise silk embroidered with cherry blossom and butterflies in gilt thread. So different from my old tartan blanket that smelled faintly of dog, bought by Mum for 10p from a car boot sale.

Jamie and I could not believe our luck. Every day we roamed through the house, always discovering new treasures. We had favourites which changed almost every hour as we found something else that caught our attention and aroused our interest.

One day, three weeks after we'd moved in, Jamie and I were playing in the attic. We weren't supposed to be there as Grandpa and Mum had both told us it was out of bounds. Grandpa was worried because he didn't quite know what we would find if we were allowed to explore. I think it was because he couldn't remember half of what was stored there.

Of course, that was its attraction for Jamie and me. We didn't usually like disobeying Grandpa, but he was out and Mum was washing her hair, and somehow we dared each other up the stairs and into that huge, gloomy space under the roof.

There were boxes and bags and chests and suitcases, stacked and piled up all over the floor, as alluring as buried treasure. I was instantly drawn like a magpie to an open jewellery box with glittering diamanté spilling out in casual disarray, as if someone had arranged it artfully for a still-life photo. As I slipped the too-big bracelets over my skinny wrists, Jamie stood next to me, poking around in a tin chest.

'Mia! Look what I've found.'

Humming happily and trying to fasten a pearl choker around my neck, I turned to see. The pearls slipped from my hands like water as I realized that Jamie was pointing a gun at me.

'Is it a *real* gun?' I asked in awe. I don't remember being frightened. I *do* remember thinking that the pale grey revolver with its silver inlay was beautiful.

'I don't know.' Jamie pointed the gun at me, holding it with both hands. He tried to squeeze the trigger, but couldn't. 'Bang, bang! You're dead, Mia!'

I collapsed gracefully against the tin chest, clutching my heart, and Jamie roared with laughter.

'Let me have a go,' I said.

Jamie ignored me. He was examining the trigger more closely. 'It's broken,' he said in a disappointed voice. 'It doesn't work.'

'Jamie, let me *see*!' I demanded.

I snatched the gun from him. It felt cool and smooth to the touch, and the weight and shape of it in my hands was completely alien and therefore completely fascinating.

I aimed the gun at Jamie. I tried to press the trigger as he had done, but it didn't move. 'Bang, bang!' I said. 'Now *you're* dead!'

'Urrrgh!' Jamie gurgled. He staggered melodramatically around the loft, clutching his side. 'You got me!'

A footstep on the stairs outside. Jamie and I turned,

guilt written large all over our young faces.

Mum appeared in the doorway, wearing her old dressing gown, her hair wrapped in a red towel. She saw the gun and her scream nearly brought the roof crashing in on us all.

'My God, Mia, what are you *doing*?'

Mum dashed across the loft, almost tripping over the hem of her dressing gown. She snatched the gun from me and held it gingerly, carefully, dangling it from her index finger by the trigger, holding it away from us and away from herself as if it might go off of its own free will.

'Where did you find this, Mia?' she demanded. 'Guns are very dangerous – you could have been killed! You're a very, very naughty girl, and I'm going to tell Grandpa exactly what you've done. He'll be very angry with you.'

Tears welled up in my eyes. I didn't want Grandpa to know that I'd disobeyed him.

'Jamie found the gun,' I blurted out, pointing my finger accusingly at him. 'It was all *his* fault.'

'Tell-tale,' Jamie muttered.

Still holding the gun at arm's length, Mum glared at Jamie, who was standing sullenly beside me.

'Then *you're* very naughty too, Jamie,' she snapped. 'Now get downstairs where I can keep an eye on the pair of you.'

I don't know what happened to the gun. I don't even know whether Mum told Grandpa what had happened because, although I waited with dread for the inevitable scolding, he never said anything. Maybe Mum kept the gun for her own reasons. Or maybe she just hid it and forgot about it. I don't know.

But now I remember that last year Jamie mentioned the gun again. It was just after Grandpa died. Mum wanted some old junk from the loft to sell at a car boot sale and Jamie and I were poking around up there and he said quite casually, 'Do you remember when I found the gun?'

'Yes,' I replied. 'Mum had a fit.'

'Well, I don't think the gun *was* broken.' Jamie was packing leather-bound books in a cardboard box, turned away from me so I couldn't see his face. 'I think the trigger was stiff, that's all, and we were too little to squeeze it properly. It was actually loaded too. Did you realize that, Mia?'

I shook my head. At the time I didn't think anything of it. But now that remark comes back to haunt me.

Does it mean that Jamie found the gun again and has tested the trigger since that long-ago day when we first found it in the loft?

Four

Shivering, nauseous, I am still sitting on the stack of *Macbeth*s, wondering what the hell I am doing here. The noise has stopped. It didn't happen gradually, it was quite sudden, like someone flipping a switch to turn it off. It seems that everyone, in this part of the building at least, has left, and I am alone.

'It's not too late,' I tell myself aloud. 'I can still leave.'

I climb to my feet with an effort, like a shaky old woman. I take one step towards the door and then freeze, immobile, as I hear footsteps running down the corridor outside. They echo loudly in the empty building.

A teacher checking that everyone has left?

The gunman?

Jamie?

Are the last two one and the same?

What are you going to do now?

Don't hang about.

Make a decision.

Making decisions has never been my strong point.

But I stumble behind one of the bookcases where set texts for English Lit classes are stacked. The space is narrow and I stand with my back pressed against the wall and my face against dusty copies of *To Kill a Mockingbird*.

Then the cupboard door opens and I am so shocked, I almost wet myself.

I do not move or make a sound. But through the slatted bookshelves I can see my form tutor, Ms Powell, standing in the doorway.

I can leave, I say silently to myself. All I have to do is step out from behind this bookcase right now. Ms Powell will take me outside and I'll be safe.

Do it.

Do it now.

I don't move. I am as still and silent as if I'm in my grave.

Ms Powell is of African-American origin and ebony-skinned, but now she looks grey with fear. She glances quickly into the cupboard and then runs away, leaving the door open.

My knees buckle and sag. I totter out from behind the bookcase and nausea overtakes me. I'm gut-wrenchingly sick, all over a stack of copies of *Hamlet*.

I don't much care because I never liked that play. Almost all the characters are either mad or murderers.

I lean against the wall and wipe my mouth and try to think straight. I've made the decision to stay, but I have no idea what to do next.

Focus, Mia.

With an enormous effort of will, I force myself to admit that I have already made my decision.

'I must find Jamie,' I murmur aloud. 'That's what I have to do.'

For the first time, as I walk shakily towards the open door, it occurs to me that if the gunman and Jamie are *not* the same person, then I could be in serious danger. But from now on, I guess I have to assume that they are. I have to, because I've put myself willingly into the middle of this utterly terrifying situation. And if they are *not* . . . ?

I sideline the thought of possible dangers. I am – almost – sure that it *is* Jamie. But I do think of Mum, and I have to take a deep, trembling breath.

I step out into an empty, gloomy corridor. The black blinds are drawn all the way down to block the low-level winter sunshine on one side of the school, the side that faces the entrance gates, the playground and the car park, and for this I give silent thanks. No one outside can see me.

There is a ghostly pall hanging over the building. All the classroom doors stand open, and as I walk by, my legs shaking, I see overturned chairs and books on the floor, interactive whiteboards left on and all the signs of a frenzied rush to evacuate the building. Occasionally a mobile phone left behind in a locker rings and makes me jump. I strain my ears for the sound of gunshots, but I hear nothing.

Where am I going? I ask myself as I stumble down the stairs.

I don't know. When I last saw Jamie, he was heading

towards the annexe. The annexe is over on the other side of the school, as far away as it could possibly be from where I am now. As I reach the bottom of the stairs, I am on the ground floor of the huge extension that was built onto the left wing of the school. The annexe is way over on the right-hand side.

But Jamie might not be in the annexe at all. He might have gone there first and then moved on somewhere else. He and Grandpa's gun – and the hostages – may now be in a different part of the school altogether.

I simply don't know what to do. Should I search every part of the school or just go straight to the annexe? Frowning, I agonize over a decision that could be a matter of life or death, literally. Then, as I pass the library door, I am suddenly and sickeningly aware of voices in the eerie silence, voices drifting towards me from further down the corridor.

'Oh, God,' I gasp, almost sliding to the floor as my knees threaten to give way beneath me.

Half of me is glad that perhaps a teacher – Ms Powell or someone else – is looking for me. Half of me is petrified that it might be Jamie and a gun.

Jamie wouldn't hurt *me*, I'm sure of it.

But would he hurt others?

If I *honestly* believe that he was involved in events that have happened in the past, then there can only be one answer.

I can't hear footsteps, just voices, and I strain to hear what they are saying; after a moment I realize that something doesn't sound quite right.

Silently, just in case I am wrong, I move along the ground-floor corridor towards the staffroom, a few doors down from the library.

I step inside very cautiously, in case someone's there. But as I suspected, the TV in the corner of the staffroom has been left on, forgotten about in the rush to escape. Two women are discussing, in hysterically over-interested voices, the latest unlikely happenings in *EastEnders*.

I am disappointed.

I am relieved.

I don't know *how* I feel.

I turn to leave, feeling suddenly uncomfortable in a room where pupils are never allowed. As if any of the teachers would care, today of all days. But that's the idiot that is me, Mia Jackson. My twin brother might be in school with a gun, and I feel guilty about doing something I shouldn't—

'*We interrupt this programme to bring you some breaking news. Unconfirmed reports are coming in that a school in Birmingham is being evacuated after a gunman entered the building. Police have been called to the scene.*'

Nausea rises in my throat again and I turn back to look at the TV. My eyes meet those of the newsreader, who is blonde and beautiful enough to be a Hollywood actress.

'*There are further unconfirmed reports that a class of Year Nine pupils and their form teacher were missing from the emergency roll-call, and may be trapped in the school's annexe, possibly being held hostage by the gunman.*

'*It is believed that an armed response unit and trained negotiators specializing in siege situations are also on their way to the school. More news as we get it.*'

My mind races as the screen flips back to the two women on their sofa. But one thought stands out, clearer than any other: *I must go to the annexe.*

An undiluted, intoxicating burst of sheer adrenalin shoots through my veins. Somehow I have to get to the annexe, to Jamie. I can do it. I *must* do it. Despite the differences between us over the last year, Jamie is still my brother and I still love him with all my heart, and I will not allow him to do this terrible thing for my sake. I do not want anyone injured, or worse, in my name.

I pull off my school sweatshirt and tie it around my waist. Then I wrench off my tie. I'm about to drop it when I stop and wonder if it might come in useful. So I loop it around my skirt on top of my belt instead. I roll up my sleeves, take an elasticated hair band from my pocket and scrape my hair back.

I am ready.

Strangely, I haven't felt so alive in months. Perhaps years.

Every nerve in my body singing, I run full tilt out of the door, down the corridor and round the corner.

There I bump, hard, into Ms Kennedy.

Five

I have no idea when I first realized that Jamie was different. I know that it took me a long time to see it because we were the same in so many ways. We were babies together, tucked up in our pram, sharing the same blanket. We learned to walk and talk at the same time. We finished each other's sentences and could often read each other's minds, in the way twins sometimes can.

But over the years I gradually came to understand, with a vague, unspecified feeling of dread, that Jamie wasn't like me. I didn't have the wild streak that was so much part of his character. Jamie's favourite words were *I dare you, Mia,* and when I double-dared him, he would go even further than I'd suggested and get himself into extraordinary, dangerous situations.

Once Jamie dared me to open the window of my bedroom, three floors up, and lean right out into space. It sounded scary to my six-year-old self, so I immediately double-dared *him* to open the window and then stand on the ledge. I could have bitten my tongue off even at the very instant I was speaking because Jamie immediately bounded over to the window and flung it open without a trace of fear.

'Watch this, Mia,' he said.

He climbed up onto the narrow ledge and stood in the open window, the breeze lifting his hair. He leaned forward a little, then glanced back over his shoulder and gave me a cheeky grin. By this time, of course, every nerve in my body was taut with panic.

'Get down, Jamie!' I wailed, putting my hands over my eyes. 'Get *down*! I'm telling Grandpa!'

But when I took my hands away again, Jamie had vanished.

I was fixed to the spot for a couple of minutes, too terrified even to scream. Whispering his name, I peered outside, heart palpitating, expecting to see a crowd of people gathered around a crumpled, broken body lying on the pavement.

But there was no body, and the passers-by were simply going about their ordinary business. Then, suddenly, someone was behind me, and I did scream this time. There was Jamie, his black eyes glittering triumphantly. He had inched his way along the outside ledge, high above the traffic, to the open window of the next room, climbed in and then strolled back to surprise me. There were other incidents like this, too many to count. But when, years later, I told Jamie how much he'd frightened me, he just laughed.

'I feel really alive when I do dangerous stuff, Mia,' he told me. 'It's a buzz, an adrenalin rush. You should try it sometime.'

But Jamie isn't just reckless with his own safety.

I think he's hurt other people too.

I have no proof and I've never asked him about the things I suspect. It's so much easier to say nothing.

Michael Riley could have been the first. I say *could* because I have no proof, you understand.

A few months after we moved in with Grandpa, Jamie and I started nursery school. It was Grandpa's idea and Mum took a whole lot of persuading. But, at last, off we went, two mornings a week for three hours at a time, to paint, model playdough and mess around with sand and water. I think Grandpa was hoping that mixing with other children would help Jamie and me to separate from one another a little and become more independent.

But it didn't work. I loved the toys and the activities, but I was wary of the confident, outgoing little girls with their Barbie backpacks and outfits colour-coordinated with their hair accessories; their bright, chatty, friendly mums who were nothing at all like my own. I kept myself to myself, and I only ever played with Jamie. Of course Jamie wasn't overawed by anyone or anything at the nursery, but he only wanted to play with me too.

The boys all ignored me except a redheaded one called Michael Riley. To this day I have no idea why, but he took an instant dislike to me. It began with him tipping a cup of water onto my shoes. He put sand in my orange juice and a snail in my coat pocket. For some reason he seemed to be on a mission to search out every possible way he could torment and tease me. I hated him, and Jamie hated him even more on my behalf.

'Now, what would you like to do this morning?' Lisa asked on our fourth visit. Lisa was one of the nursery nurses, blonde, comfortably plump, with a calm, reassuring voice. 'Some of us are going to make paper flowers. Would you like to join in?'

I glanced over at a table covered with coloured tissue paper and pots of glue. Michael Riley was hovering around it, brandishing a paintbrush like a sword. He stuck his tongue out at me and crossed his eyes.

'No thank you,' I said. 'Jamie and I would like to play in the Wendy house, wouldn't we, Jamie?'

'Yes, please, Lisa,' said Jamie, smiling widely at her. He took my hand and gave it a squeeze.

Lisa sighed a little, but she was too kind to insist. 'OK, off you go,' she agreed, and we skipped off hand in hand.

Inside the red and yellow Wendy house, Jamie busied himself with the ironing while I stood at the plastic stove and cooked the dinner.

Suddenly a hand sneaked through the gap in the gingham curtains. My ponytail was grabbed and pulled eye-wateringly hard, making me cry out. I caught a glimpse of Michael Riley's grinning face as he ran off and I burst into tears of shock and pain.

Jamie dropped the iron and ran over to me immediately. 'Don't cry, Mia,' he said, sliding his arms around me.

'I hate that Michael Riley,' I sobbed. 'And now I've burned the sausages.'

'Never mind.' Jamie patted me on the shoulder. 'I'll go out for a Domino's pizza. You lay the table.'

Left alone in the Wendy house, I dried my tears on the checked tablecloth and began to put out plastic plates, cups and cutlery. The ritual of laying the table, something I always did at home with Grandpa, calmed me, and I began to sing to myself.

Suddenly I heard an ear-splitting scream. And then I saw Michael Riley lying on the floor outside the Wendy house, very still. His arm was twisted underneath him at a sickeningly awkward angle.

Lisa and Beth, the other nursery nurse, were on the scene immediately. As the other children crowded round, demanding to see, I stayed where I was. I remember thinking that it served Michael Riley right for being mean to me. I didn't realize then that Jamie was nowhere to be seen.

Michael Riley was unconscious when the paramedics turned up and took him away on a stretcher. We heard later that he was fine, apart from having broken his arm in two places. Apparently Michael had been pushed, hard, from behind and hadn't seen his assailant as he fell. Lisa and Beth and Mrs Ransome, the owner of the nursery, asked every one of us if we had seen what happened. We all denied it, and it never occurred to me then that maybe Jamie wasn't telling the truth.

Mrs Riley was furious about Michael's injury. She tried to sue the nursery, although that came to nothing. So even when his arm had healed, Michael did not come back, and I didn't have to put up with his teasing any longer.

I never asked Jamie if *he* was the one who pushed Michael over. It didn't even enter my head at the time, and then when I grew older and it *did* enter my head, I didn't dare ask.

It could all have been so innocent. Jamie and

Michael could have been fighting and Michael could have slipped. Maybe Michael hadn't wanted to tell his mother that he'd been involved in a fight. And so he'd lied and said someone pushed him.

There was no reason, though, why Jamie couldn't have told *me* the truth.

But Jamie never mentioned Michael again.

Maybe it seems like a giant, unbelievable leap to go from that to this, to what's happening here today.

But Michael Riley was only the beginning.

Six

All the adrenalin rush, all the determination, all the bravado that had sent me racing off down the corridor drains away, as if someone had picked me up and wrung me out like a wet cloth. I just stand there, unable to move, gawping at Ms Kennedy as if I've never seen her before.

Ms Kennedy looks equally shocked. Her hands fly to her face, her mouth falls open and her eyes are round, completely circular with surprise. She looks like *The Scream*.

But it's Ms Kennedy who recovers first.

'Mia! *Mia!* What in God's name are you doing here? Why aren't you outside with everyone else?'

Ms Kennedy is even blonder and more beautiful than the newsreader. I have hero-worshipped her ever

65

since she was my Year Seven form tutor. She's now my English teacher and I love her fun and interesting lessons. Ms Kennedy is not only gorgeous and well-groomed, she's intelligent and witty and writes poetry which is published in glossy magazines. I envy her. I'd like to *be* her.

'I don't know, miss,' I mumble feebly as I try to collect my shattered wits. I'd been so sure that this part of the school at least would be empty after all this time. Then, with a shock, I realize that it's probably only about ten minutes since Ms Powell checked the cupboard where I was hiding. But every crazy, emotional roller-coaster of a moment seems like an hour right now.

Ms Kennedy ignores me. 'Come with me immediately, Mia.' She grasps my arm and begins to pull me with frantic urgency towards the nearest exit. 'We *must* leave right now. I was just about to go myself. We had to round up some *idiotic* Year Ten kids who sneaked back into school to get their phones from their lockers.' Ms Kennedy shakes her head in disbelief, still gripping my arm. 'But I think everyone's safely out now.'

Docile as a lamb, I hurry down the corridor with

her in the opposite direction to the way I was going, back past the staffroom and the library. Away from the annexe. I am used to doing what teachers tell me, so I obey automatically. Maybe it's for the best, I think. Perhaps I can be of more help to Jamie on the outside.

'Is it true, miss?' I ask, still hoping for the answers that have eluded me so far. 'Is there really someone with a gun in the annexe? Who is it?'

'I don't know, Mia.' Ms Kennedy abruptly speeds up so that we are now running down the corridor together, hurtling breathlessly round the next corner. 'No one knows. Let's just get out of here, all right? Then we can find out exactly what's going on.'

'But *why* does no one know anything?' I complain.

I am about to blurt out my fears about Jamie, but a strong self-preservation instinct immediately kicks in and I restrain myself. Ms Kennedy appears to know nothing and I don't want to say anything about Jamie because I don't want to put ideas into people's heads, just in case the mysterious gunman *does* turn out to be someone else. It's still possible.

And, my God, who knows what might happen if I

start making wild claims about Jamie that later turn out to be untrue? Things could get very complicated and unpleasant indeed.

I'm not going to allow *anyone* to break up my little family, sad and dysfunctional unit that we are. I'm not going to allow Jamie himself to smash us apart either.

Not if I can help it.

Ms Kennedy does not answer. She is as fiercely intent on the emergency exit ahead of us as Bree was earlier.

'How did the rumour start if no one knows who the gunman is?' I continue as we fly down the long, long corridor towards the double doors. 'Who set off the alarm? Why—?'

Ms Kennedy makes a sound that is halfway between a moan and a shriek. 'For God's sake, Mia, *shut up!*' she screams.

I am utterly shocked. I come to a sudden halt and wrench my arm from Ms Kennedy's grasp. I've never heard her yell like that before, not even in class.

Ms Kennedy whirls round to face me. She is ghostly white and panting hard. I realize that she is utterly terrified. For once I have the upper hand because I am *not*.

'What are you doing, Mia? Come *on*, you stupid girl!' And she plunges forward to grab my arm again.

But I jump backwards, away from her.

I suddenly understand the role that Ms Kennedy has played in this situation. She definitely has to take some of the blame. It was *she* who persuaded me to enter the essay competition. Fine, that wasn't her fault, I was quite willing. It was a national competition and I won.

First prize. Two hundred and fifty pounds worth of book tokens for the school, and a hundred for myself.

Then, last week, the headteacher, Mr Whitman, read my winning essay out in assembly to the entire school, without telling me he was going to do so. It was meant to be a surprise and it certainly was, but not a pleasant one because my essay was intensely private and personal. I could have died of embarrassment. In fact, it would have been a relief at the time.

Ms Kennedy claimed that she didn't know what Mr Whitman was planning either, but I wonder if that was true. After all, she got a lot of praise for persuading me to enter the competition. I can guess exactly what the other teachers were saying.

Isn't Natasha Kennedy wonderful? Look how she's brought that quiet, pathetic little mouse Mia Jackson out of her shell . . . Imagine her writing a prize-winning essay!

It's entirely possible that Ms Kennedy is one of the people who have used and abused us and, like Jamie, I am sick and tired of it. I have had enough – *enough* – of everyone telling me what to do.

Pure adrenalin sings through me once again. But this time it's fuelled by intense, all-consuming rage. A rage I didn't even know I was capable of feeling.

'Mia!' Ms Kennedy lunges at me again and then almost howls with frustration as I step sideways to avoid her. 'Don't be a bloody idiot! Come *on*!'

'No,' I shout.

I evade her clutches, turn and race back down the corridor, away from the exit. I am quick, but Ms Kennedy is quicker. I forgot she is a star member of the school's running club and has competed in the London

Marathon three times. She catches up with me at the corner and clamps my shoulders in a vice-like grip, spinning me round towards her. She slaps my face, not hard, but enough to make me gasp. My eyes sting and I am momentarily thrown off-balance.

'Calm down, Mia, and don't be a fool!' she shouts. She grabs my arm and begins to drag me back towards the exit again.

'Let go of me!' I shriek, lashing out at her with my free hand.

We begin to fight, Ms Kennedy trying to dodge my flailing arm and pull me back towards the exit, me still hitting out at her and trying to break free.

I cannot believe I'm fighting with a teacher.

But I am desperate. Almost instinctively, I stamp hard on Ms Kennedy's foot; she gasps in pain and her grip on me loosens slightly. I take advantage of this to give her a hard shove.

I swear I didn't mean this to happen, but Ms Kennedy staggers backwards, slips on the polished floor and goes down. She hits her head on the protruding window ledge as she falls, then blacks out. She lies there motionless as I gaze down at her in abject horror.

Oh God, now I've killed a teacher.

Tears streaming down my face, I sink to my knees beside Ms Kennedy. I grab her wrist and try to check for a pulse, but I have no idea what I'm doing. I look around frantically for help but of course there's no one here. What now?

Then, with a sob of relief, I see Ms Kennedy's eyes flicker. She mumbles something but then sinks into unconsciousness again. I can see now that her chest is rising and falling with every breath. She is definitely alive, thank God.

I scramble to my feet to flee, but hesitate. I am free to go to Jamie, but I can't leave Ms Kennedy here. She might be in danger, and I can't have that on my conscience. My nerves stretched like elastic to breaking point, I stand there wondering what to do next.

Then, out of nowhere, there is a loud burst of classical music, and I'm so frightened I almost have to scrape myself off the ceiling. It takes me a couple of seconds to realize that Ms Kennedy's mobile phone is ringing.

I bend down, take the mobile out of her jacket pocket – it's the latest designer must-have – and glance at the display screen. *Keisha Powell*. My form tutor.

I am about to press the *off* button when suddenly I realize that here is the answer to my problem of what to do with the unconscious Ms Kennedy. Instead of turning the phone off, I press the answer button.

'Hello? *Hello?*' Ms Powell is already yelling at the other end of the line as we are connected. 'Natasha, for God's sake, where *are* you?'

'Hello,' I mumble.

I think about trying to disguise my voice but the best I can do is to speak very low and quietly.

'Natasha, the police are moving us right away from the school,' Ms Powell shouts, hardly waiting for my reply, her usually calm and measured tones touched with hysteria. In the background I can hear all kinds of noise – shouts and screams, car engines and the unmistakable sound of people weeping. 'They want to know why you haven't come out yet. The armed police are going to be here in ten minutes. You have to get out of there *now*—'

'Ms Kennedy is lying in the corridor near classroom Seven B,' I cut in. I am gabbling wildly because I am so desperate to get this information across. 'She's OK, but she had an accident and hit her head and she's unconscious. Someone will have to come and help her.'

Without waiting for a reply, I fumble to switch the phone off. But I'm not quick enough and Ms Powell comes through loud and clear.

'Who *is* this?' she demands, her voice sharpening. 'What's all this about an accident?' There's a pause and in my panic to cut the connection as fast as possible, the phone almost slips through my trembling fingers.

'Oh, God!' I mutter. 'How do I turn this thing off?'

There is an intake of breath from Ms Powell at the other end of the line. 'Mia! Is that you? Where are you, and—?'

The phone goes dead as I finally manage to find the right button to cut the call. But almost immediately it begins to ring again. Swearing and sweating and shaking uncontrollably, I finally manage to work out how to turn the phone right off, and there is blessed silence as the display screen goes dark. But now everyone, including the police, will know that I'm still in the building. Maybe by now they have also discovered the identity of the gunman.

I untie my sweatshirt from around my waist, roll it into a pillow and slide it gently under Ms Kennedy's head. Then I replace the phone in her pocket. At first I think about taking it with me. I haven't had my own phone for months because we couldn't pay the bill, and it might be useful if I need to ring Mum or Bree. Or maybe the police.

But vague fears of being tracked by the phone signal on my way over to the annexe stop me. So I leave the phone behind.

I take a last look at Ms Kennedy; I hope that she will be all right and that someone will come for her very soon.

As I run off down the corridor I try to recapture that rush of heady adrenalin from before, but all I am feeling now is real, undiluted fear.

This time there is no going back.

Seven

I want you to understand that Jamie is not a monster.

I'm telling you about things that he *might* have done when we were younger. Maybe he did them, maybe he didn't. Like I said before, I don't have proof of any kind.

Perhaps it was just a coincidence that our Year Two teacher, Mrs Merriman, had her handbag stolen the day after she scolded me for talking to Jamie in class. She was so harsh and so cutting, I was completely crushed and humiliated. The school caretaker was blamed for stealing Mrs Merriman's bag, amongst other things, and he was sacked. Nobody liked him, he wasn't a nice man, so it all made perfect sense and everyone was satisfied.

But a secret doubt still lingers.

And there might have been other things.

I am *sure* there were other things.

Mr Culpepper was one of our neighbours, and he was very proud of his garden. Grandpa told us that Mr Culpepper always won prizes for his plants at the local gardening show, although I much preferred the blowsy, tangled mass of wildflowers, grasses, butterflies and bees in our garden to the regimented blocks of colour next door. Jamie always said that Mr Culpepper hid in his kitchen with a water pistol, ready to blast out of existence any insects that had the cheek to stray into his garden.

Mr Culpepper did not like children. He kept any of our footballs that accidentally went over the fence between our gardens and burned them on his bonfire. When my special bubblegum-pink I AM 6 birthday balloon escaped, the string sliding through my hot little hand, it floated next door and Mr Culpepper burst it with a needle. I sat down on the back doorstep and cried so much that eventually Jamie gave me his own blue balloon to cheer me up. Meanwhile Mr Culpepper sprayed his roses with insecticide, looking grimly pleased with himself as he destroyed hundreds of greenfly.

A month later, Mr Culpepper's plants began dying, turning into rotting brown stems before our astonished eyes. It was the talk of the street, and Grandpa and Mum were sure that Mr Culpepper had been sabotaged by one of his gardening rivals. Jamie and I simply thought that it served him right. Eventually, though, I did feel sorry for Mr Culpepper when I saw him crying over a beautiful coral-coloured rose tree that was shrivelling and dying. Mr Culpepper didn't bother with the garden again after that. He moved away a few months later and we never saw him again.

At the time it never entered my head that Jamie might – *might* – have had something to do with this. I only realized later that in the jumble of the old, collapsing shed at the bottom of our garden, there were several rusty cans of weedkiller.

But could Jamie actually *do* such a thing?

Would *any* six-year-old?

I know the 'normal' ones wouldn't.

And there were other happenings too.

It would take me a long time to tell you them all. They mean almost nothing on their own, but if you put them together and look at them as one, they appear more than slightly sinister.

These were the happy years, though, living with Grandpa. There was always food on the table and hot water for baths in the old claw-footed Victorian tub, and the electricity never got cut off because Mum hadn't any money for the meter, and we didn't have to hide whenever anyone came to the door in case they wanted payment for something or other. Jamie and I had always felt responsible for Mum, but now we were safe with Grandpa because he stepped in and took charge of her illness.

'Your mum needs some help because the chemicals inside her body don't always work the way they're supposed to, the way ours do,' Grandpa explained to Jamie and me. 'It's not her fault, always remember that.'

After months of persuasion, Grandpa managed to get Mum to see the doctor. Then, using a variety of methods, he would alternately wheedle, beg, blackmail or bully her into taking her medication regularly. At first Mum refused and would flounce off in a rage, but Grandpa never gave up.

'Come along, my darling,' he'd say, stroking Mum's hair, and eventually she began dutifully taking her tablets, like an obedient child. Grandpa also tried to persuade her to start seeing a therapist, and she did, in a fitful kind of way.

But, very gradually, the highs and lows of Mum's behaviour began to stabilize, and Jamie and I saw someone different, someone we hardly recognized as our mother, someone who wasn't either severely depressed or outrageously overconfident and full of her own self-importance. It was all very slow, and there were times when Mum slipped back into her old ways. But I was so much happier, and so was Jamie. I had always been much closer to Mum than he was, but now he would draw pictures for her at school or make breakfast or leave a flower on her pillow.

Normal things.

Suddenly we were a normal family.

Remember what I told you? When something good happens to me, something bad follows right on behind? When Jamie and I were twelve years old, Grandpa became very ill, and a year of hospital visits began.

'Grandpa has cancer and the doctors don't know if he's going to get better,' Mum explained. She was tearful when she told us, but the melodramatic outbursts that were such a feature of her illness were now a thing of the past. 'And he has to stay in hospital for a long time.'

There was a poster on the wall of the hospital visitors' room where we spent so many unhappy hours, waiting for the latest update about Grandpa's condition. *One in four people will get cancer in their lifetime*, it said above a picture of a blonde white woman, a young black man, an elderly Asian lady and a middle-aged man. As Grandpa became thinner, more yellow-faced and shrunken, I used to wonder who the other three people in the world were who wouldn't get cancer now that my grandpa had it. I had to try hard not to hate them.

The operations and the chemotherapy did not work and just after our thirteenth birthday, Grandpa came home to die. He lay in his bed, silent, unmoving and unblinking, sinking in and out of drug-addled consciousness. He didn't seem to recognize us most of the time. My heart felt as if it had shattered and I couldn't imagine it healing again, not ever.

'Why does Grandpa have to die?' I asked Mum. 'It's not fair.'

She and I were curled up together in one close, loving embrace under a patchwork throw in front of the living-room fire. I hadn't seen Jamie since we got home from school, but I guessed that he was upstairs with Grandpa. Jamie spent a lot of time just sitting silently next to Grandpa's bed; even in his drug-induced stupor, Grandpa seemed to like having Jamie close by.

Mum sighed and rested her chin on the top of my head. 'Life isn't fair, darling. But we'll never forget Grandpa. We'll keep him alive in our heads and in our hearts.'

I was silent. That just wasn't enough for me. The thought of never seeing Grandpa again was frightening and unbearable, and tears dripped down my face and ran off the end of my nose. We cried together until our eyes were sore. Then Mum, exhausted from late-night vigils, fell asleep, and I carefully crawled out from under the throw and slipped upstairs.

Grandpa's bedroom was warm and slightly stuffy, with the smell of sickness hanging in the air like thick fog. The lights were dimmed, but Jamie was there, sitting patiently beside the bed, as always. Together we looked down at Grandpa's slight, still figure hidden under the mound of bedclothes.

'He's sleeping,' Jamie whispered. 'Where's Mum?'

'She's asleep too,' I replied. 'She's worn out.'

'Has she taken her tablets?'

'*Yes*, Jamie, she has.'

Jamie was always on Mum's case, and it annoyed me. Mum was doing fantastically well. Even during Grandpa's illness she'd kept taking her medication and she'd been strong, even in the midst of coping with her own grief. She had even promised that she would never allow her illness to take control of her again. Why couldn't Jamie accept that Mum was all right now, I thought, frustrated, and just get off her back?

At that exact moment Grandpa's eyes suddenly snapped open. He glanced at Jamie and me without any sign of recognition in his dull, unfocused gaze.

'I'm here, Grandpa,' I said softly. 'It's Mia. You remember me, don't you? Shall I fetch Mum?'

Grandpa did not reply. I wasn't even sure he could hear me. His red-rimmed, glazed eyes were fixed on Jamie and me as if he wasn't quite sure who he was looking at. It was strange, like he was seeing us clearly for the first time.

'It's all right, Grandpa,' I said as, panting and groaning, he struggled to pull his old, withered frame into an upright position. Jamie and I both tried to ease him gently back down onto the mass of pillows. But Grandpa shook us off irritably.

'What's the matter, Grandpa?' Jamie asked.

A gurgle rose in Grandpa's throat as he tried to speak and a chill ran through me at the look on his face. His eyes bulged from their sockets and his mouth was slack, a thread of saliva dribbling from it.

'It's all right, Grandpa,' I said quickly. A shiver trickled along my spine as I saw that he was very frightened, and I rushed to reassure him. 'Don't be frightened. I'm Mia, and this is Jamie. You remember Jamie? He—'

Grandpa gasped for breath. He dragged his eyes from Jamie and stared into mine, gripping my hand with his last remaining strength.

'Jamie,' he whispered, so low I could barely hear him. 'Mia. Be careful—'

And then he died.

I can still see that look on Grandpa's face.

Be careful.

To this day I'm still not sure what he meant.

Was he going to say something about Mum to Jamie and me?

Or was he warning me about Jamie?

Had Jamie confessed something to him during the long, long hours he spent in the sickroom?

Did Grandpa know something terrifying that I didn't?

I have no idea. But within six months of Grandpa's death, everything had changed. Grief-stricken, Mum broke her promise and stopped taking her medication and her illness quickly took a vice-like grip on her once more. I had no one to turn to except Jamie, and this was when our relationship started to break down: for some inexplicable reason he turned from me and began pushing me further and further away.

I think that was when he first began to follow, faster and faster, the downward spiral to self-destruction.

Eight

Monday 10 March, 9.22 a.m.

Sweating, panting, I race to put as much distance between me and Ms Kennedy as possible. I hope she's going to be all right, but she is not my biggest problem right now. According to Ms Powell, the armed response team – and that means police who have guns – will be here in ten minutes.

Less, now.

So in around eight minutes or so there are going to be marksmen surrounding the school, and I will be in even more danger.

'Don't think about it,' I repeat to myself over and over again as, heart thundering in my chest, I run back the way Miss Kennedy and I have just come. As I pass the staffroom once more, the TV is still murmuring in the silence, but I resist the temptation to go back and check the latest update. I don't need the TV reports: there is breaking news going on right outside, only a few metres from where I am now.

All I have to do is stop and look.

I stop.

I tiptoe into the nearest classroom, go to the window and position myself directly behind the blind. As it's made of thick black canvas, there should be no giveaway shadow visible on the other side, nothing to tell the police that I am here.

There is a very small gap between the edge of the blind and the window recess and I put one eye to the gap and look outside, clinging to the blind to keep it from moving aside and betraying me.

'Oh, *Christ*.'

There are eight – no, ten – police cars parked in the distance outside the school gates. There are police officers, too many to count, milling around in the street. Some of them wear riot gear, body armour and hard helmets with face protectors. I can't see any guns, though. I am still safe from the armed police for a short and ever-decreasing period of time. There is no one else around, no pupils, no teachers, no watching crowd, no faces at the windows of nearby houses. Everyone has been moved away from the school, as Ms Powell said.

For the first time I begin to wonder how the police will handle the situation. Almost instantly, a memory surfaces of myself and Jamie watching TV just a few months ago. A man with a gun had barricaded himself into a flat in – Leeds? Liverpool? Somewhere like that. He had a hostage, his ex-girlfriend, with him and the armed response team were called in. But the police began by negotiating with the man, and this went on for two days.

'They'll talk, to begin with,' I reassure myself, remembering that news story. 'They won't just rush straight in and start shooting.'

I wonder briefly if what we saw that day planted the seed of an idea in Jamie's mind. The siege ended when the man let his ex-girlfriend go, but killed himself with a single shot.

I gently release the blind and let it settle back into place. As I do so, I hear the shriek of an ambulance on its way. I wonder if this has been called for Ms Kennedy or if it was coming anyway, in case there are any casualties.

I want Ms Kennedy to be all right, I really mean that.

I don't hate her. I hate *myself*.

I should have listened to Jamie months ago, and maybe then this wouldn't be happening.

But it is happening, and this is how you've chosen to deal with it.

Be strong and get on with it.

I shoot off down the corridor again. I am now leaving the extension behind me and am in the original school building. I pound my way past the school office, the headteacher's study, the school hall.

I am coming closer and closer to the annexe.

I wonder what is happening there.

I wonder what Jamie is doing right now.

And Kat Randall.

Will she be as quick to open her big mouth in front of someone who has a gun?

As I take a short cut through the DT department, I glance through an open doorway and see tools laid out for a woodwork lesson. Chisels, hammers, Stanley knives, drills.

I skid to a halt. I have just thought of something earth-shatteringly important that I haven't even considered so far.

If I need to defend myself at any time, in any way, I have nothing.

Nothing.

No self-defence skills.

No weapons.

How satisfying it would be to reveal at this moment that behind my meek and mild-mannered appearance I am a karate black belt and a master of kung fu. Sadly, though, I *am* actually meek and mild-mannered. I have never chopped a block of wood in half with my bare hands. I can hardly tear an envelope open without getting a paper cut.

I hurry into the DT room and grab a large and a small chisel and a Stanley knife. Then I weigh the hammers in my hand, much as I weighed the gun all those years ago in the loft, searching for one that's big enough to inflict damage, but not too heavy to carry around with me.

'But would I actually have the guts to use it?'

I wonder aloud.

Another flash of recent memory.

Thursday, a few weeks ago, and Jamie and I were sitting in the form room before the bell for morning lessons. Ms Powell does not subscribe to the view that her class should be allowed to do whatever they want in the fifteen minutes between registration and lessons, be it gossip, read *Heat* magazine, arm-wrestle or whatever. She structures the time so that we have silent reading on Mondays, Wednesdays and Fridays (*Heat* magazine definitely not allowed), and a discussion about stories in the news on Tuesdays.

Thursday is philosophy day. We come into class to find a question written on the whiteboard that is guaranteed to provoke debate. On the day I'm thinking of, the question was:

Do you think everyone has the capacity to kill another person, if they are provoked far enough?

'No,' I said definitely, when asked for my opinion. 'No, I just couldn't do it.'

Usually I am so torn between the opposing sides of the question that everyone in class, including Jamie-

and Bree, gets annoyed with me. My trouble is that I can see both sides of every argument and, as I told you, I hate making decisions.

This time, though, I was completely and utterly sure. I could never hurt anyone in that way, whatever they'd done to me.

'Not even in self-defence, Mia?' Bree asked, and I shook my head.

Most of the girls agreed with me, although some said they would have no problem if they had to kill to escape a man who was attacking them. The boys were less sure, although the majority of them were also quite convinced that the only reason why they might kill was in self-defence.

'I think it depends on your attitude to yourself,' Jamie said quietly when the debate had got very heated. 'If someone doesn't feel that their own life is worth very much, or maybe nothing at all, then that someone won't value other people's lives very much either. And that makes him or her dangerous.'

Was Jamie talking about himself that day?

His words come back to haunt me as I choose a

hammer and add it to my self-defence kit. I bundle the tools into a plastic carrier bag I find lying on the teacher's desk and then I tie the handles of the bag to the belt around my waist, leaving my hands free.

Maybe *I* don't value my own life much, I muse as I run from the DT department. After all, I've chosen to put myself in the middle of this life-and-death situation, haven't I?

And if Jamie's right, does that makes me more dangerous than I realize?

I am close to the annexe now, so close I can almost smell my own fear. I wonder what is happening in there, in Class 9D's form room. I wonder if everyone is still alive.

I run faster. Ahead of me I can see the double doors that lead into the long, L-shaped glass corridor, the corridor that connects the main school to the annexe. My heart thumps faster.

But as soon as I push my way through the swinging doors, I realize that I have made a mistake.

A stupid, *stupid* mistake.

I have assumed that all the blinds at the front of

the school are pulled down. Here they are not. For a second I stand there in the corridor in front of the large plate-glass window, totally exposed to whoever happens to be looking in from outside.

'Oh, God!'

I drop to the floor so fast that I almost stab myself in the side with the tools that hang around my waist. There I freeze, the pale, clear winter sun blazing through the window, burning my eyeballs. Trembling from head to toe, I glance up, expecting faces to appear. I wait in limbo for the glass to shatter as the police come in after me and drag me to safety.

But nothing happens. So I take a deep breath and pull myself together. Then, adjusting the bag of tools so that it sits behind me, I begin to inch forward on my stomach like a paratrooper in the jungle.

After a moment, when still no one comes, I dare to believe that I have not been spotted after all.

I edge my way along the short leg of the L-shape, and then round the right angle. Relief floods through me as I see that, in this longer stretch of corridor leading to the next set of double doors, the blinds on the playground side are drawn.

I still don't stand up, though, until I am near the doors. At last, after what seems like an eternity, I inch right up to them. Trembling, I drag myself upright, hanging onto the door handles for support.

Behind these double doors is the annexe.

Behind these doors, on the first floor, is 9D's classroom. Kat Randall is there. And Jamie? I don't know what I will find, but nothing will make me turn back now.

I push gently on the swing doors, expecting to slip smoothly through into the annexe.

The doors do not open.

They are locked.

Nine

After Grandpa died, I gradually realized how much Jamie had begun to hate Mum.

Actually, it would be more truthful to say that Jamie hated her illness, rather than Mum herself. But because it was so bound up with Mum's personality and the way she behaved, it was difficult to separate the two. Jamie had always blamed Mum a whole lot more than I did for not taking the necessary steps to try and control her condition, but when Grandpa had gone and she had stopped taking her tablets again and slithered headlong back into depression, Jamie became even more frustrated.

'This is ridiculous, Mia!' he would shout, pacing up and down the living room. The fury that poured out of him paralysed me with fear, and I would sit there in silence, too afraid to say anything. 'We know that she behaves differently when she takes the medication, so *why* won't she take it?'

I had asked Mum this very same question myself when Grandpa was ill, when we were close and could talk more easily than we'd ever done before. But Mum had looked so upset, so desperately ashamed and embarrassed, that I wished I hadn't asked at all, and I said so.

'No, Mia.' Mum put her arm round me as I stood there, hanging my head, unable to look into her eyes, which were so, so sad. 'You deserve an explanation. It's just . . .'

She paused, thinking very deeply for a moment before she spoke again.

'When I'm in that hyper state, it's so marvellous, I can't tell you. I need hardly any sleep or food and yet I have so much *energy*. It's euphoric. It's exhilarating. I feel like I can do anything and no one can hurt me. It's like *flying*.' She laughed nervously. 'I know it's difficult for you to understand, Mia. But I feel so special. I feel invincible.'

I was silent, I remember. I tried to imagine an illness that could make you feel that way, but it was impossible. Wasn't being ill supposed to make you feel – well – *ill*?

'It's so hard to give that feeling up,' Mum sighed.

'But what about the other side of it?' I asked, desperate to make sense of something that seemed so unbelievable. 'The depression? The days lying in bed, crying? Surely you don't enjoy that too?'

Mum shook her head. 'Of course not. Then I feel like I'm stuck at the bottom of a deep, dark hole and there's no way for me ever to climb out. But that's the payback, Mia. It's a trade-off, one for the other.'

I told Jamie all this, a few months after Grandpa's death when Mum's behaviour was changing once more. But Jamie's attitude did not soften.

'If Mum wants to do whatever she likes, then she shouldn't have had kids, should she?' he retorted, his face set and hard, determined not to try and understand. 'She never thought about *us*.'

'That's simplistic, Jamie,' I argued. 'Life doesn't always work out like that.'

'And don't I know it?' Jamie had muttered, turning his back on me.

It's never easy to look back and see where a problem situation began, but I would guess that this moment marked the beginning of the breakdown of the relationship between Jamie and me. We'd always had each other to depend on, and I could rely on Jamie for support, but suddenly he seemed to be working to a completely different agenda. He withdrew completely, both physically and emotionally, washing his hands of Mum and her illness and the day-to-day problems it caused, and yet he kept on and on nagging *me* to do something about it.

We struggled on for months after Grandpa died, although I found it increasingly hard to leave Mum at home when she was in a depressive state. I ended up taking the odd day off school to keep an eye on her. Jamie refused to help. Mum sometimes talked about ending it all, which completely terrified me, but I don't think she'd ever actually tried it. It was perfectly possible, though, that she'd attempted to harm herself in the past and Grandpa had kept it from us.

The manic side of Mum's behaviour seemed to be getting worse. She was out all day spending money we didn't have, and then out all night clubbing. In desperation, Jamie stole and hid Mum's credit cards, but a few days later she was out shopping again. I told Jamie she'd found the cards. The truth was, I gave them back because I felt so sorry for her. I know I'm a fool, and Jamie knew it too. He was raging, but this time he was furious with me rather than Mum. He disappeared that Friday night and didn't come back till late on Saturday afternoon. Mum was out partying and she didn't come home either.

So I sat on my own in that dark, tumbledown old house, absolutely terrified that neither of them would ever come back and I'd be left on my own.

Jamie was first to return. I was desperate to be cool and restrained, but when I saw him, I burst into noisy tears of relief. At one time Jamie would have comforted me straight away, but not now. He stood watching me with a strange, unreadable look on his face.

'I thought you weren't going to come back,' I gulped.

'One day I might not,' Jamie said soberly.

That was the very first time he said it.

Mum eventually came home too, but her wild and reckless lifestyle continued. I was hardly getting any sleep, waiting for her to come in every night. For God's sake, Jamie and I were supposed to be the teenagers, not her.

'This stops *now*,' Jamie said savagely after we'd walked into the kitchen and found a strange man in his underwear, making tea, for the third morning in a row. The man looked extremely embarrassed, dropping the hot tea bag he'd just fished out of the mug onto his bare foot.

'Sorry, didn't realize there was anyone else here,' he'd mumbled, hopping around the kitchen clutching his burned toe. Then he'd fled upstairs to Mum's room to collect his clothes.

'This stops now,' Jamie had repeated, staring at me challengingly. 'Mum *has* to go back to the doctor, Mia.'

I tried to keep my face neutral and not show what I felt. I was tired and I was worried and I just wanted everything and everyone to go away and leave me alone. I wanted Jamie to deal with it all. But I had already realized that my instinctive negative reaction to everything, my immediate conviction that I could not and would not cope, was beginning to irritate Jamie intensely.

For some reason, he seemed to *need* me to show him that I had a backbone.

'She won't go.'

'She has to,' Jamie replied curtly, staring me full in the eyes. 'Or they'll have to come here and see her.'

'She'll run off and hide.' I tried to stare right back at him but could not stand his searching gaze. So I pretended to examine my fingernails. 'Anyway, you have to be dying for a doctor to make a house call these days.'

'OK, then, we'll get her to the surgery somehow.' Jamie did not intend to give in. 'For God's sake, Mia, can't you see that things can't go on like this?'

'But you know what will happen, Jamie,' I said wearily. 'Mum won't go. And even if by some miracle, she agrees and says yes to the medication and yes to the therapy – well, she just won't take the tablets and she won't turn up to see her counsellor and everything will go on exactly the same way as before. It took Grandpa *years* to get Mum to do those things.'

'Let's worry about that part later.' Jamie's eyes were glittering strangely. They looked almost manic, which reminded me uncomfortably of Mum. 'There might be ways we can get her to see reason. Just make an appointment with Doctor Fields, Mia, and we'll take it from there.'

I nodded. I was too exhausted and beaten down to argue.

'Make the appointment but *don't tell Mum when it is*,' Jamie said quietly. 'At least then we'll have the advantage of surprise.'

We had to wait a few weeks until the autumn half-term holiday because it was difficult to get an appointment out of school time. But finally I managed to make the appointment for the Monday of half-term week at 9.30 a.m. At 8.45, Jamie and I went into Mum's room. She was lying on her back, sleeping.

'Mum.' I went over to the bed, took her shoulder and shook her gently. 'Wake up.'

She did not move or open her eyes.

'Mum!' I shook her again, but again, nothing. I glanced up at Jamie, fear racing instantly through me. 'Jamie, you don't think—'

Jamie pushed me aside. He gently moved Mum's hair away from her face and studied her intently.

'No, Mia, it's all right. Look, she's breathing.' He picked up an almost-full bottle of pills from the bedside table. 'What are these?'

'I don't know,' I said. 'I've never seen them before.'

Jamie read the label on the back of the bottle. Immediately his face darkened in fury.

'Sleeping pills.' He slapped the bed in frustration. Mum didn't even stir. In fact, she gave a gentle little snore as if confirming what Jamie had said. 'Forget it, Mia. We'll never wake her now.'

'But where did she get the pills from?' I asked.

'You can buy any old crap over the internet these days.' Jamie shoved the bottle into his pocket. 'You don't need a doctor's prescription.'

'We don't have the internet—' I began.

Jamie clicked his tongue in annoyance. 'God, Mia, do you know *anything*? Mum goes to the library and uses the computers there. That's how she meets all these guys, through online dating sites.'

'How do you know that?'

'I followed her, of course,' Jamie retorted with a scowl. 'I've been spying on Mum for months.'

I was silent for a moment. It would never occur to *me* to do such a thing. But then, Jamie is single-minded and ruthless and always, *always*, one step ahead of me.

'Well, what do we do now then?' I asked. I had a secret, sneaky sense of relief that we no longer had to try and persuade Mum to do something she hated. Anything for a quiet life, that's me. Even if that life is almost unbearable.

Jamie did not answer. But the accusing look on his face made my heart sink.

'Did you tell her, Mia?'

'Tell her what?' I blustered.

'About the doctor's appointment today.' Jamie's eyes were cold, hard, glossy chips of ebony. 'Did you tell her? Is that why she took the sleeping pill?'

'I did *not* tell her,' I said truthfully.

But Jamie knows me all too well.

'Did you write it down anywhere?' he demanded.

'I—' My cloak of bravado fell away, leaving me exposed. 'I put it in my diary.'

Jamie gave me a look. 'Get your coat,' he said, and walked out.

'Why?' I chased out of the room after him. 'Where are we going?'

'To see the doctor.'

'But there's no point, Jamie.' I was still repeating the same thing over and over again as we reached the surgery car park, even though I was pathetically grateful that he'd taken charge of the situation. 'The doctor won't tell us *anything* about Mum. Medical confidentiality, remember?'

'I don't *need* to know anything about Mum,' Jamie replied, striding ahead of me through the car park. 'I've lived with her illness for the last thirteen years. What I want to know is what the hell they're going to do to help.'

When I'd phoned to make the appointment, the receptionist had told me that Dr Fields – jolly, charming, grey-haired Dr Fields – had just retired unexpectedly early, due to ill-health, and a locum called Dr Caroline Zeelander would see Mum.

Dr Zeelander didn't exactly inspire confidence in me. She was elegantly tall and at the very extreme of skinniness. She looked like the horrific photographs of anorexics I'd seen in magazines where the skin barely seems to cover the bones. Her blonde hair was scraped back severely, showing every skull-like plane and bone of her face.

'You are *not* Mrs Annabel Jackson,' was the first thing Dr Zeelander said as she stared at me with the pale green eyes of a pedigree cat. She did not say hello or any other words of welcome.

'Sorry, no, I'm not,' I apologized. 'Mrs Jackson's my mum. She couldn't come—'

Instantly Dr Zeelander whipped round and closed down the open page on her computer. I suppose Mum's medical records were on the screen and we weren't allowed to see them.

'Then may I ask what you're doing here?' Dr Zeelander asked coldly. 'The appointment's in your mother's name. Didn't you tell the receptionist that your mother wasn't with you?'

Nervous at being caught out, I glanced at Jamie, but he simply shook his head very slightly.

'Er – we told her Mum was outside making a phone call,' I blurted out anyway. I didn't dare look at Jamie, but I could sense his immediate annoyance with me. 'Sorry.'

'Stop apologizing, Mia,' Jamie said irritably. He glanced at Dr Zeelander, who looked utterly outraged. 'The most important thing is to explain why we're here—'

'Please leave,' Dr Zeelander cut in crisply. She went over to the door and opened it. 'If your mother needs to see me, she has to come herself. I won't discuss her case without her being present.'

'But—' Jamie began.

'Please go. Now.'

I don't really know why, but I got the feeling that Dr Zeelander was stretched as taut as wire. There were faint blue shadows under her eyes and her hands were shaking slightly. I don't think it was anything to do with us. How could it have been? But I also got the strange impression that she was almost *enjoying* what was happening, that asserting her authority was somehow giving her a much-needed sense of power.

I glanced at Jamie. His face was suddenly very white and pinched, his black eyes burning coals. He was so angry, he was almost giving off sparks.

Then, with one brief, swift movement, Jamie lashed out with his left arm and swept the in-tray piled with files and documents off Dr Zeelander's desk. It crashed to the floor, scattering sheets of paper everywhere.

Jamie grabbed my hand and dragged me over to the door. There he stopped, right in front of Dr Zeelander. He was almost as tall as she was, and their eyes met, Dr Zeelander's huge and disbelieving, Jamie's cold, ice-cold, and filled with raging frustration. Then he pulled me out of the consulting room.

Dr Zeelander was frozen to the spot with shock and made no attempt to stop us. I glanced back as we left the surgery and saw her still standing there, mouth open, shaking from head to toe. I couldn't blame her. The sheer, brutal force of Jamie's anger, displayed so openly, had frightened me to death too.

'You've never done anything like that before,' I muttered as we crossed the car park. Jamie was so full of adrenalin he was half running. I could barely keep up with him. 'What if Doctor Zeelander tells—?'

'Shut up, Mia,' Jamie snarled at me. Anger was still flooding out of him, so blazing and white-hot it was almost tangible. I had never *seen* him like that before. He had never shown that side of him to anyone, even me. 'She won't tell, and anyway, what does it matter if she does? There weren't any witnesses except you. That snotty bitch deserved it, and more.'

The following day I was in the Spar minimarket at the end of our street, and there a sentence on the front of the local newspaper leaped out at me with sickening clarity. *Doctor's car vandalized – police appeal for witnesses. See page 4.*

It wasn't the main story, it wasn't even a big headline, but somehow it was almost like I'd been waiting for it. Like I'd been expecting it.

As if in a dream, I saw my trembling hands reach for the newspaper and turn to page 4.

DOCTOR'S CAR TARGETED BY VANDALS

Police today appealed for witnesses after a local doctor's car was wrecked by vandals. Dr Caroline Zeelander, a locum at the Waterford Surgery in Kenwright Road, found her car – a new silver BMW 5 series with the distinctive numberplate ZEE 1 – had been targeted yesterday when she left after evening surgery to drive home. Not only were the car's headlights smashed and the tyres slashed, but a tin of red paint had also been poured over the entire vehicle.

'This was a vicious attack,' commented community PC Rehana Patel, who was first on the scene. 'It's possible that this is a random act of vandalism, or it could be someone who has a particular grudge against Doctor Zeelander, we just don't know yet.'

PC Patel went on to request that if anyone saw anything of the attack, believed to have taken place between 6 and 8 p.m. on Monday evening, then they should contact the police immediately. When asked about the incident, Dr Zeelander refused to confirm reports that she had taken out a restraining order against her estranged husband only the previous week.

I stood there staring at the newspaper for so long that the manager of the minimarket came to ask me if I was all right. I could barely answer him because I felt that if I opened my mouth, I might actually blurt out the terrible thing I was thinking.

Had Jamie had anything to do with the attack on Dr Zeelander's car? He'd disappeared without a word yesterday around a quarter to six. He'd come home just after eight.

It seemed so impossible, and I did try very hard to convince myself that it could not be. After all, Caroline Zeelander hadn't come across as the most sympathetic of doctors. Even though she was only working at the surgery temporarily, any of the other patients there might have had a grudge against her. Alternatively, as the newspaper seemed to be implying, it might have happened because of problems in her personal life.

But all those little incidents – Michael Riley and the others – had lodged themselves deep in my subconscious over the years and very gradually, almost without me acknowledging or even realizing it, I had come to accept that Jamie was – well – volatile. Dangerous.

And the memory of the venomous rage, driven by frustration, that he had directed at Dr Zeelander still made me gasp. The helplessness he felt in dealing with Mum and – be honest, Mia – with *me* was pushing him to breaking point.

And I could not stop asking myself this question.

How far would Jamie dare to go?

Ten

Monday 10 March, 9.35 a.m.

'*No!*'

I stand in front of the locked doors that bar me from entering the annexe, my whole body a pantomime of complete disbelief. My eyes are wide, my mouth falls open, my fists are clenched.

I push at the doors again more violently, shoulder-charging them, but it's useless. They are definitely locked.

It never occurred to me that this would happen: during school hours the doors at both ends of the L-shaped glass corridor always remain open. They're only ever locked at night. I guess that, as the school was evacuated, a teacher or maybe the caretaker thought it might be a good idea to contain the potential threat posed by the gunman while everyone escaped.

117

Even as these thoughts race through my mind, which only takes about two seconds, I am aware that I don't have time to stand and think.

Because if I'm going to make it into the annexe before the armed police arrive, somehow I have to get these doors open.

I wrench the plastic bag of tools from my waist. My first crazy thought is to use the hammer to smash my way through the wooden panels at the bottom, but I realize instantly that this would make a loud noise. So instead I grab the largest chisel and begin trying to jemmy one of the doors open.

I am the most inept burglar in the whole world though, because however hard I bear down on the chisel, even with all my weight behind it, nothing happens. The door does not move a single millimetre.

I am too angry and too fired up even to burst into tears, which is my usual coping technique in a crisis. I realize that there is only one way I'm going to get into the annexe, and it is not through these doors.

Instead I must go outside and find another way in, out of view of the police.

And then I hear it. The sound of a vehicle arriving at the school gates. I don't bother to draw the blind aside a little to look because I already know what it is.

The armed police are arriving.

Somehow I have to get out of the glass corridor and into the annexe before I am spotted, apprehended or shot.

I have only two choices.

One is to return the way I've just come, into the main school building, and then out through the exit near the DT room. From there I can run along the back of the school, past this glass corridor where I am now, and into the annexe through the back entrance.

'Will I have time?' I mutter to myself, still levering at the doors with the chisel, still making little or no impact on them.

Or will the armed police swarm silently around the building and catch me?

There *is* another way out of here. I am not at all athletic, but I think even I can manage this.

Slipping the chisel back into my bag, I turn to my left, to the large plate-glass windows opposite the ones that have the blinds drawn. The white-painted window ledges are broad and low, almost like window seats, and I jump up onto the nearest one.

Then I reach up to the long, rectangular window above the bigger bottom sheet of glass that does not open. I unhook the latch.

The window swings open and fresh, frosty air hits my face, sending a stream of invigorating energy through me. I grasp the bottom of the frame and heave myself up, my trainers scrabbling for a foothold on the smooth expanse of glass below.

I pause for breath and then manage to swing one leg up and out of the window. I sit astride the frame painfully for a second or two, and then I swing my other leg out. Slowly I let myself down to the ground on the other side. There's no broad window seat outside, only a narrow ledge, so I have to drop further than I would like.

I land on my knees on the gravelled flowerbed under the window, scraping holes in my thick black tights and cutting my hands. But I am out.

Yes!

I can't shout the word aloud, but I punch the air in triumph.

I turn to my right, back towards the annexe. Keeping close to the building, I edge my way along the length of glass corridor to the side wall of the annexe which juts out beyond it. I press myself nervously into the shadow of the building and take a couple of breaths.

Then, glancing nervously from side to side like a frightened bird, I slip sideways and round the corner of the annexe.

There I stop and look up. I am almost directly below Class 9D's form room on the first-floor corner of the annexe. I know the classroom well. I had French lessons there when I was in Year Eight.

But I can see nothing because the blinds are drawn. In fact, I note that the blinds are drawn at all the classroom windows at the back of the annexe. I hope that no one is standing watching me right now, peering round the blind as I watched the police myself a few minutes ago.

Wondering what I am doing and how to stop me from doing it . . .

Hugging the wall, keeping flat, I scuttle as fast as I dare to the back doors, which are about halfway along the building. Every second I expect to hear a shout of *Stop!* Maybe even *Put your hands in the air and don't move!*

But I hear nothing and see nothing.

Gasping with relief, I reach the back doors of the annexe. I push them but they do not move. These doors are also locked.

'Oh, God, I don't believe it!'

Dropping my head into my hands, I clutch wildly at my hair. Now I am seriously panicking.

Think.

I know the school like the back of my hand.

Find another way in.

Almost crazed with tension, my last remaining bit of common sense telling me to give up and give in, I look along the back of the annexe. I dare not attempt the fire escape because that is right round the corner, on the side wall of the building, and would put me at grave risk of being spotted by the police.

Nor can I see any windows open on the ground floor

of the annexe that would allow me a way in. But a little further along, right at the far corner, is the flat-roofed, single-storey extension that was added to provide extra cloakrooms for those pupils whose form rooms are in the annexe. When I glance upwards, I can see that one of the tiny first-floor windows above the flat roof is open, just a sliver of a gap. I rack my brains and realize that it is a window into the girls' lavatories.

It is my only chance. First, though, I have to climb up onto the flat roof.

I feel an urge to burst into hysterical laughter and almost have to slap my own face to calm myself down.

How the hell am I going to do that? I wonder.

Climbing up onto the flat roof is a much more difficult proposition than getting out of the window in the glass corridor. There are no broad window-seat type ledges for me to balance on. The cloakroom windows have narrow ledges that look barely wide enough for a foothold.

But nevertheless I know I'm going to try.

I choose the window closest to the drainpipe that

runs from the flat roof to the ground. Grasping the ledge, I haul myself onto it, clinging to the drainpipe for support.

As I suspected, the ledge is too narrow for me to balance my feet on properly. Cursing under my breath, wobbling precariously, I try to hold onto the drainpipe, but its smooth round surface makes it difficult to get a good grip.

Still teetering on the ledge, I pull my tie from my waist and loop it around one of the drainpipe's brackets. Then I hang onto it. Having something to hold onto means I can balance on the ledge a little more easily.

Once I have stopped wobbling quite so much, I stretch upwards, straining every muscle to extend my arms so that I can grasp the edge of the flat roof.

'I only get one go at this,' I whisper to myself as I flex my fingers. I know there is a strong possibility that, if I don't haul myself up at my first attempt, I will unbalance myself and fall backwards off the window ledge.

I push all thoughts of falling, hitting my head on solid concrete, breaking bones, out of my head. I let go of the tie as my hands close on the edge of the flat roof, and then I push upwards with all my might. My feet flail in thin air for a moment and then I find a toe-hold on the window frame.

I manage to raise myself a little higher than the edge of the roof and then pitch forward so that I fall flat onto my stomach. A surge of triumph rushes through me as I scramble awkwardly up onto the roof.

For a moment I stand there, hands bleeding, savouring my success. Then I realize that I am a sitting target and drop hastily to my knees. The flat roof is filthy, covered with dead leaves and punctured footballs and, strangely, a single old and battered Nike trainer.

I reach over the edge and pull my tie free of the drainpipe. Then, keeping low, I shuffle over to the window that I noticed from below. Unfortunately it looks even smaller than I first thought.

'Am I actually going to get *through* there?' I ask myself doubtfully.

I won't know until I try.

And once again, I'm not exactly overwhelmed with other options.

I try to slide my fingers into the narrow gap at the bottom of the window to push it upwards, but it's a tight fit. So I take out the small chisel. The end of the chisel slides smoothly into the gap, fitting perfectly.

Then I push on the handle of the chisel as hard as I can and the window jerks up a little way. I drop the chisel and now my fingers will fit underneath the window and I can lever it up. I exert all my strength, and the window moves up, once, twice more. Then it sticks again and all my efforts won't move it a single centimetre.

I bite the inside of my cheek anxiously as I stare at the gap. It's wider than before, but I'm still not really sure if it's big enough for me to get through.

Here I go.

I push my bag of tools through the window and drop them gently onto the floor of the lavatory cubicle below me. Then I follow, head first. The gap is small and I'm panicking already. I manage to get my shoulders through and suddenly I am halfway in.

I put my hands on the cold white china of the toilet cistern just below me and take a breath. Then I begin to wiggle this way and that to get the rest of me through the narrow space.

But nothing happens.

I strain and I push and I heave, but I do not move. It's just like a comedy film, except that this is not funny in any way.

I'm like a cork in a bottle.

I am stuck fast.

Eleven

I'm a coward, as you know, and I didn't say anything to Jamie about my suspicions. But for the next few weeks I checked the local newspaper every day to see if the person who wrecked Dr Zeelander's car had been caught. In fact, I almost got banned from the minimarket because I was in there every day after school, leafing slowly through the paper, scanning every page intently but buying nothing.

But I never saw anything more about Dr Zeelander. So what did I do then?

I simply tried to forget all about it.

And yet, in the deepest, darkest, most remote corners of my mind, those places where we dare not go in the light of day, *I absolutely believed that it was Jamie. That he had returned to the surgery with revenge in mind, and had taken out his fury with Dr Zeelander on her car.*

I could deal with this terrifying thought fairly successfully by keeping busy and refusing to think about it. But it would surface with relentless, agonizing regularity in the middle of the night and keep me awake for hours.

I did not *want* to believe it.

But I did.

So where did I go from here?

Well, *nowhere*.

What could I do?

I had no proof of anything and Jamie was my twin brother and I loved him and I needed him. He was the only person I could lean on and even if his support was waning, I was clinging on tenaciously because it was all I had.

'What do we do now?' I asked Jamie the day after I'd read the newspaper report. I did not mention it, of course. I would have cut my tongue out first. Nor did I say anything about what had happened in Dr Zeelander's office because I knew instinctively that Jamie would not talk about it.

'Excuse me?' Jamie said politely, as if I was some

kind of crazy stranger who'd accosted him in the street. 'What do we do about *what*?'

I stared at him in perplexity. 'Well – Mum, of course.'

Jamie pressed his fingers to his temples as if he was in pain. 'How many times have we had this conversation before, Mia?' he murmured, still in the same polite tone. 'Let's go through the options again, shall we? We could ring Social Services—'

'*No*, Jamie.'

As far as I knew, Social Services weren't aware of our problems as we'd lived such a stable life with Grandpa for the last eleven years or so. And I wasn't even certain that we would be a high priority for them, anyway. I mean, it wasn't as if Jamie and I couldn't take care of ourselves and Mum wasn't dangerous or abusive. Not *really*. She yelled a lot and threw things, but she'd never been violent. We had food and we had a roof over our heads.

On the other hand, I always had a terrible, lurking fear that, if Social Services got involved, they would find some way to split us up.

Jamie sighed. 'What are you so afraid of, Mia?'

'I don't want to be taken into care,' I cried. The tears came fast, as they always did, but I swallowed and gulped and managed to hold them back because I knew how much Jamie hated my weakness. 'I don't want to run that risk.'

'All right,' Jamie conceded. 'You'd have to toughen up anyway. Right now you wouldn't last five minutes in care on your own, Mia.'

'But I wouldn't be on my own,' I said quickly. 'You'd be with me.'

Again, that strange, enigmatic look on Jamie's face. 'I am *not* going into care,' he stated with frightening certainty. His eyes were as black and as fathomless as the night sky as he looked away from me. 'What about Mrs Francis?'

'The school counsellor?'

'Yes.'

I shivered violently at the very idea. 'I don't want *anyone* at school to find out about Mum.'

I meant the other kids. I could all too easily imagine their comments. Some of the teachers knew about our situation, but I'd never told them that Grandpa had died, and I knew Jamie hadn't either, so I expect they assumed that everything at home was still all right.

'Then the only way is to make Mum go back to the doctor and get her started on the treatment again,' Jamie replied impatiently. 'Then even if the doctor tells Social Services, at least Mum will be back on the happy pills and it's much less likely that they'll do anything drastic. And we are *not* seeing that useless cow Doctor Zeelander again.' He smiled coldly, secretively, to himself and I had to look away. 'Ask for someone else.'

'But Mum won't go to the doctor so then we're back where we started—' I began in that dispirited, *poor-little-me* tone that I knew drove Jamie to utter distraction. But I couldn't help it.

Jamie shook his head. 'No, we're not.' His clenched knuckles were white, betraying the tension within him, belying the casual calm of his voice. 'Because this time we're going to do it differently.'

'How?' I asked, mystified.

Jamie shook his head. He was supernaturally

calm, scarily so. 'I don't know yet,' he replied slowly, consideringly. 'I have to think about it. We might only get one chance at this, and so it has to be *right*.'

I couldn't breathe. I felt as if I was hurtling into a dark, airless tunnel and there was no way out, no light at the other end. 'I'm frightened, Jamie.' This time I *did* start to cry, I couldn't help it. 'Tell me what the hell you mean.'

Jamie did not reply. I wasn't sure he'd even heard me.

'You – you won't do anything without telling me f-first?' I stammered and stuttered to get the words out as he strode over to the door. 'Promise me, Jamie? Promise me!'

My words hung in the air as Jamie left the room. He did not promise. He didn't say anything at all.

Jamie's cryptic words had made me desperate. I had no idea what he was planning, but I guessed it would be something crazy and reckless, something that would surely be dangerous for all of us, including Jamie himself.

How could I stop him?

I tried everything I could to get Mum to see a doctor.

I begged and pleaded and wept to no avail. I didn't know why, but Mum had what amounted to a phobia about doctors and surgeries and hospitals, and nothing I said made a blind bit of difference.

In the middle of all this, I almost cracked and asked Ms Kennedy for help. One Friday morning just after half-term she asked me to stay behind after an English lesson, and when everyone else had gone she placed a leaflet on her desk in front of me.

UK Young Writers' Essay Competition.
Win hundreds of pounds worth of book
tokens for you and your school!

I remember I looked up at Ms Kennedy, puzzled.

'I'm showing this to a few select pupils,' she said, a slight smile on her lips. She nodded encouragingly at me. 'You're one of them, Mia. You know what a talented writer I think you are. You must enter.'

I picked up the leaflet, but I didn't read it straight away. Instead I studied Ms Kennedy for a second or two. She was beautiful and glowing, and even though she was just about old enough to be my mother, I felt drab and dull, frumpy and thick-witted in comparison.

One day Ms Kennedy would have beautiful, intelligent children and she would be the perfect mother, kind and caring and sympathetic, interested in everything her sons and daughters did or said. I wondered how it would feel to have a mother like that. Someone you could confide in.

'Well, what do you think, Mia? You have plenty of time – the closing date isn't for a few weeks yet.'

The moment for confidences passed as I thought better of it. I read the leaflet instead.

Write an essay of no more than 1,000 words on the following subject: 'My Life and the People Most Important to Me'.

Writing the essay was a challenge I took on gladly. I had no thought in my head of winning, but it gave me something to focus on besides my daily battles with Mum and my fears about what Jamie might secretly be planning.

But by the time the essay was finished, I'd had an idea.

Tossing and turning sleeplessly in bed every night, I had suddenly realized that there was one person left who *might* help us without wanting anything in return or putting in motion what might turn out to be dangerous consequences. It was a very long shot, but it was the only one I had left.

Jamie and I knew nothing about our father, not even his first name, and we'd never tried to find out either. But it proved remarkably easy once I set my mind to it. While Mum was out late at night – and, as often as not, Jamie too – I was feverishly searching the house, looking for anything about our father that would help me to track him down. At the very least, it gave me something to do besides sitting and worrying about both Jamie and Mum.

I knew only a pitifully small amount of facts, gleaned from the occasional unguarded remarks that Mum and Grandpa had made about him. I knew that he was originally from Birmingham, like Mum, and that they'd moved to London after they were married. They had divorced and my father had left London for somewhere else. That was it. To start searching for him, I would need his full name.

It took me a few weeks, but one evening I was sorting through the huge antique mahogany bureau that had belonged to Grandpa when what I was looking for literally fell into my lap. A crumpled but official-looking document tumbled out of the pages of an old address book and my own name leaped out at me.

Mia Katherine Jackson.

I'd never seen it before but I knew it was my birth certificate. I smoothed the paper with trembling fingers, wondering if my father's name would be there. It was:

Father's name: *Leo Dominic Jackson.*
Occupation: *Graphic designer.*

Then an address in London, the place where Mum had been living when Jamie and I were born, I thought. But by that time my father had left London altogether.

Maybe he had gone back there since. I hoped not. It would take me about ten years to save up the money to go to London.

Or maybe he had come back home to Birmingham as Mum had done.

I would start with both possibilities.

I did not tell Jamie what I was planning. I wanted to show him that I was strong enough and capable enough to do something about our situation. I wanted him to be proud of me.

Or maybe it was because, somewhere in my subconscious mind, I had already realized that this could be one huge disaster.

I spent long hours in the local library, copying down the addresses and phone numbers of all the L. D. Jacksons who lived in London and in Birmingham. That took me several weeks. Then I sold some of Grandpa's beautiful Chinese bowls of paper-thin porcelain to a second-hand shop in order to get the money to make the phone calls. I hated doing it but I had no choice.

So whenever Mum and Jamie were both out, I would go to the phone box at the bottom of our street and call the next name on the list.

'*Hello, I'm looking for Leo Dominic Jackson.*'

'*Sorry, love, no one of that name here.*'

During the Christmas holidays I worked my way through the London names and then started on the Birmingham ones. I knew that Leo Jackson might be anywhere. He might have emigrated, he might have died. But at least this gave me the feeling that I was doing something, however futile my quest might be.

And then, just after we'd returned to school in January, when I'd begun to think I had no real hope of ever getting anywhere, I called a number in an area on the other side of Birmingham.

'Leo's not here,' said a soft female voice with the faintest twang of a transatlantic accent. 'Can I take a message?'

I cut the connection because I immediately felt sick and dizzy. My head swam and I thought I might faint; I grabbed onto the sides of the telephone box for support. Up until this very moment, crazy as it sounds, I had been concentrating on how I could help Mum, how I could show Jamie that there was some other way we could get out of this situation, believing that maybe our father would be the key to it all. I hadn't really thought much about what it would be like to meet my dad for the first time after so many years.

But now my heart was slamming against my chest, my stomach churning, my nerves shot to pieces. These physical symptoms of my fear were bad enough, but I couldn't understand what was happening inside me, to my emotions. I was a bubbling, seething, indescribable mass of terror and elation.

The next Saturday morning I slipped out of the house to cross the city to Leo Jackson's address. *The Pines, Gladstone Road.* It was a cold, frosty day and the bus journey took ages. But my mind was running ahead of me so fast, I did not notice the distance.

I didn't have a plan. I didn't know what I was going to say to Leo Jackson. I didn't even know if I would have the nerve to knock on his door. Leo Jackson appeared to have a wife or a girlfriend; he might have other children. My stepbrothers and stepsisters.

Was Leo Jackson aware that I even existed? If he was, then why hadn't he been in touch for all those years?

And if he wasn't, he was now going to get a hell of a shock.

I had never been to Gladstone Road before. Every house was huge, detached, immaculate, with sweeping driveways and landscaped front gardens. BMWs, Jaguars, Mercedes, all with brand-new numberplates, crouched on the drives like armed guards.

The Pines was between The Firs and The Beeches. I stood at the edge of the drive and gazed up at the house. The expensive loops of curtains at the windows, the Japanese-themed front garden with a small pond and an intricate red and black bridge across it, the electric gates, the shiny black Mercedes and new red and white Mini parked behind it all screamed *Look! I made it! I'm rich!*

I felt sick with nerves. I doubted whether a pool of vomit on his pristine drive would endear me much to Leo Jackson. Should I leave right now? What was I doing here anyway? Why didn't I have a plan? Did I intend to march up the drive and knock on the door? How exactly did you approach your father after fourteen years? Were there any accepted guidelines?

It was all too much.

I need to think about this.

I took a shaky step backwards.

'Excuse me, can I help you?'

I turned. For one crazy moment I thought that the man standing behind me with a newspaper under his arm was Jamie. I saw the same dark hair falling over the brow in exactly the same way, the dark eyes, the tall, slim figure. I saw Jamie, and I saw myself. And I knew.

This is my father.

The polite, querying expression on Leo Jackson's face had been replaced by a sick, terrified look and the colour drained from his cheeks in a matter of seconds. He had realized who I was straight away. So he *did* know about Jamie and me.

My father and I stood there and stared silently at each other. Twice Leo Jackson cleared his throat, but was unable to speak. He managed it eventually.

'Are you Mia?'

'Yes.'

'Do you mind if we walk away from the house?'

Leo, my father, moved to take my arm and then abruptly changed his mind. He didn't want to touch me, and I didn't want him to either. 'You see, my wife – she doesn't know.'

I followed him to the end of the road. I can't remember how I was feeling. All my emotions seemed to have been numbed, encased in a giant block of ice.

We stopped at the corner, out of sight of the house.

'How's your mother?' Leo asked nervously. 'Is she . . . is she any better now?'

Things began to fall into place, and I understood exactly why Leo had left. It was all too likely that Mum's illness had ground him down into misery too, and he'd escaped to find a different life. But what about Jamie and me? He had left us behind without a thought.

'Not really,' I replied. My voice was slightly unsteady, but I was quite calm. I marvelled at my composure, as if I was standing outside my own body, watching myself be polite to this man who just happened to be my father. 'She got better when we moved in with Grandpa because he persuaded her to see the doctor.

But then he died . . .'

'So he *did* do something then.' Leo was talking to himself, not me. 'He found her in the end.'

'What do you mean?' I demanded, emotion spilling into my voice at last. I was suddenly hungry for details, eager to know everything my father knew, just to fill in the gaps.

'Your mum and I split up before we knew she was pregnant,' Leo mumbled. He looked immensely awkward and uncomfortable, as if my sudden blast of unguarded emotion had thrown him off-balance. 'She contacted me and said she was having twins. She even told me that she was going to call you Mia and Jamie.'

I was silent.

'The thing was, I'd got this fantastic new job lined up in the States . . .' Leo's voice faltered a little. 'I wanted to go, but I felt bad leaving her—'

'You could have taken us with you,' I broke in, feeling a deep and bitter rage stir within me.

My father shook his head. 'It was over, Mia.'

'Even when you knew that she was having Jamie and me?' I hated him fiercely at that moment. I had never realized that I had the capacity to hate someone so much before now. I suppose everyone has it, *if they are provoked far enough*.

'I couldn't go back.' My father's fingers clenched and his knuckles whitened. The long, slender fingers and oval-shaped nails were Jamie's, and mine too. 'But I couldn't just *go* either. I'd never met Annabel's parents because they'd fallen out with her over something or other. They didn't even come to our wedding. I tracked them down and told them what had happened and gave them our address in London. But she'd already moved on.'

'Grandpa never gave up though,' I said softly. 'We moved several times, but he kept on looking and eventually he found us. Meanwhile you dashed off to the States and your fantastic new job.'

I sensed a rush of quick, blazing anger in my father that reminded me of Jamie, even though the expression on his face did not change.

'It wasn't easy, Mia,' he said tightly. 'It might seem that way to you, but it wasn't. These things are *always* complicated, believe me.'

146

We were both silent.

I had so much inside my head, so many questions, and yet so many things I wanted to go away and think about. I didn't know where to start. There were too many years of neglect, too much misery, too much to say and not enough ways of saying it. I'm not just a physical coward, I'm an emotional one too, and it seemed impossible to begin the long, long task of attempting to forge some kind of relationship.

Anyway, did I really want to?

Did Leo?

'So what made you come looking for me?' Leo asked eventually.

The way I saw it now, I had nothing to lose.

'We need help,' I muttered. This was true – we desperately needed practical help – but I was seriously wondering if the emotional fall-out, the bit I had swept out of sight until this moment, was too big a price to pay. 'Since Grandpa died, Mum's been worse than ever . . .'

It saddened but did not surprise me to see that

Leo Jackson was panicking big time before I had even finished speaking.

'What do you mean by *help*?' He had to swallow before he could get the words out. 'If it's a question of money . . .'

I might have guessed he would offer cash. Someone who obviously had a lot of it would assume that a large cheque would be the quickest and easiest way to get rid of us.

'Money would be useful,' I said truthfully, 'but that's not why I'm here. Mum needs to go back to the doctor and be put on her medication again. And she ought to go back to the therapist, the one she was seeing when Grandpa was alive. Maybe if you could come and talk to her—?'

Leo Jackson looked extremely agitated. 'No, absolutely not.' He was so frightened, I would have felt sorry for him in any other circumstances. 'I . . . my wife knows nothing about you and Jamie. I can't tell her. I can't risk her finding out I've lied to her. She might leave me and take the kids . . .'

So I did have stepbrothers or stepsisters. Well, from

the look of the house, it seemed that they were having the perfect life, with a mother and a father who loved them.

This time I could not control the cold, hard fury that filled me up and spilled over into my voice. Maybe I was more like Jamie and Leo than I realized.

'Thanks for nothing,' I said, holding the sobs back with a steely effort of will I did not know I possessed. 'Sorry I bothered you.'

I turned and ran off swiftly. Only then did I allow the tears to fall.

'Mia!' I heard my father shouting behind me. 'Stop! We can talk about this. I'll give you money. Just tell me how much . . .'

Blood money, I thought scornfully. To salve his conscience. Why had I come? I didn't know. There was nothing for me here. Just someone else to let me down.

As I reached the next corner I was vaguely aware of someone sitting on the garden wall there. I couldn't see because my eyes were stinging and blurry, so I almost jumped out of my skin when a hand shot out and grabbed my wrist.

'Are you all right, Mia?'

It was Jamie.

'What – what are you doing here?' I gabbled, gulping, trying to pretend I wasn't crying and not fooling anyone.

Jamie shrugged. 'Looking out for you, like I've always done.' His eyes strayed past me, searching up the long road. 'He's gone, Mia.'

I looked back towards the corner where I had stood with my father. There was no one there now. Leo hadn't even bothered to come after me. I had never realized that I could feel so bitter, so very let down. But what did I expect? This wasn't the first time that Leo Jackson had abandoned me.

Jamie moved to brush my hair away from my wet face, but then he seemed to think twice about touching me, as our father had done. Abruptly he drew away and shoved both hands deep into his pockets.

'When will you learn, Mia?' he asked wearily. 'Stop looking for people to lean on. The only person you can rely on in this world is *yourself*. Leo Jackson left Mum and he left us, and you might have pricked his conscience now, but maybe he still doesn't give a damn. You can't expect anything from him.'

'He's terrified of his wife finding out.' I felt weary myself, mentally exhausted and longing to lean on Jamie for emotional support. But after that initial moment he had withdrawn from me once again and I didn't want to reach out to him and be rejected. 'He thinks she might leave him and take the kids.'

'That would serve him right.' Jamie's face was coldly unforgiving. 'Let him see what it's like to be deserted and left all alone. He deserves everything he gets.'

These words instantly filled me with dread. They were eerily similar to what Jamie had said after our visit to Dr Zeelander.

A week later, drawn by feelings I did not fully understand and also, if I am honest, because I was fearful of what might happen, I went back to Gladstone Road. I did not tell Jamie, though. Ever since my first visit I had secretly been hoping that Leo Jackson might get in touch. After all, he knew Grandpa's address. But he didn't.

That didn't stop me going back.

The Pines was no longer the beautiful, immaculate house it had once been. One side of it had been blackened by fire, the glass of the windows cracked and sooty. The front garden had been trampled and ravaged and the red and black Japanese bridge lay in eight pieces on the furrowed grass. The Mercedes and the Mini had gone.

I stopped at the gates and stared in disbelief at the scene of devastation before me. But I'm sure you're not surprised and I'll tell you something: I was not surprised either. I put my hands on the railings to steady myself as my head spun, and I *knew*.

'Are you ill, my dear?'

I struggled to turn my head to see who was speaking. An elderly woman was on her knees, weeding the elegant flowerbeds of The Beeches next door. She was looking at me with great concern.

'I'm . . . fine.' My throat was parched, my tongue suddenly felt too big for my mouth and I couldn't get the words out coherently. 'Was – was anyone hurt? In the fire?'

'Oh no, they all got out safely, don't worry.' The

woman stared compassionately at me. 'They're staying in a hotel while the insurance company cleans up and investigates the cause. Did you know them?'

'No,' I replied, flustered. 'Well, yes. A little. Do they – do they know how the fire started?'

'Not yet.' The woman was clearly unsure whether she should say any more. I didn't blame her. I must have looked like a mad person with my white face and my staring eyes and my hands clutching the gate as if I might fall and break into little pieces if I let go.

But I know that you believe, as I believed, that Jamie took out his anger and frustration violently on people who abused us and let us down. How far would he dare to go? For Jamie, there were no limits.

And now, as I crept away from The Pines that day, my first thoughts were for Mum, and for myself, as I wondered fearfully what dark and dangerous deed Jamie was planning next.

Twelve

Monday 10 March, 9.50 a.m.

I am panicking like I have never panicked before. I'm lying here on the window ledge, unable to move, my front end inside the toilet cubicle and my back end hanging down into thin air. If any policemen come round the corner of the annexe, they'll see a pair of skinny legs frantically waving about. This would definitely be amusing if it wasn't so scary.

'Oh, God, I can't breathe,' I moan.

I'm beginning to hyperventilate. There is a small space to either side of me, but there is none above or below. The window ledge is digging uncomfortably into my stomach and the bottom of the window is sitting painfully right on top of me, scraping at my back every time I try to move.

Then I have the bright idea of trying to pull myself

out of the gap again, back onto the flat roof. So I grip the window ledge and I struggle to push myself backwards but my legs just flap uselessly in the air behind me. The rest of me doesn't move, not one bit.

Now I am out of ideas and I am still stuck.

Stay calm, Mia, I tell myself shakily. *Let yourself go loose.*

It's not easy, but I steady my breathing and force my tensed muscles to relax.

Now breathe in and hold it and then push as hard as you can.

I take a long, deep breath and do not let it out. I contract my stomach muscles so much, it feels as if they are touching my backbone. Then I push, and this time I feel myself inch forward very slightly.

My belt and the thick waistband of my skirt are both adding extra bulk and are catching on the window ledge. Still holding my breath, I reach back through the tiny gap and under my stomach to undo my belt, then feed it through on one side of me, down onto the cistern. Next I fumble for the zip at the side of my skirt and manage to ease it down.

Then I wriggle and jiggle about until my skirt slips down to my knees and hangs, trapped there.

Releasing my belt and my skirt gives me the extra millimetre of space I need. This time when I push forward, I move. Painfully, bit by bit, I wriggle myself through the window, lowering the top half of my body down from the cistern to the toilet seat.

I pull my legs in after me, but my skirt slips down over my knees towards my ankles. I lunge back and just manage to grab it before it rolls over my feet and falls back down onto the flat roof.

I have done it. But it was a close, close thing and my insides seem to have turned to water. Well, I'm in the right place for that, at least.

I step back into my skirt and lock the cubicle door so that I can't be surprised by someone creeping up on me while my knickers are around my ankles. Then I sit down on the toilet and empty my bladder. The stream of urine sounds so loud that I stop, terrified, halfway through, straining my ears to make sure that no one has heard me and is coming to find me.

Soon I shall be making my way to Class 9D's form room.

And what in God's name happens when I reach the classroom door?

Automatically, absent-mindedly, I am about to flush when I realize the idiocy of what I am doing and stop myself. I pick up the plastic bag and the tools clink gently.

This makes me stop and think.

As I move closer to 9D's classroom, I have to be sure I don't make a single noise. It could mean the difference between life and death.

Reluctantly I take the tools out of the bag and leave them on top of the cistern. The only one I keep is the hammer, the one that will be most useful if I need to defend myself. I consider carrying it in my hand as I go, but decide this might look too aggressive.

Besides, I won't need to defend myself against Jamie, will I?

So I slip the hammer back into the bag, and I tie the handles to my belt again.

I unlock the cubicle door. I am about to step out

– I think I can allow myself not to waste time washing my hands, just this once – when I hear a noise in the corridor outside and my heart booms in my chest.

Footsteps.

Two people.

Are they coming for me?

The footsteps stop at the door of the toilets.

Who are they?

Friend or foe?

I have no way of knowing.

So right here, right now, *everyone* must be considered an enemy.

I make decisions with lightning speed.

I briefly wonder whether to lock myself in the cubicle again, but if they're simply coming to use the toilets, then it will look incredibly suspicious if one door is locked.

Very gently, with the tip of my index finger, I push the door so that it half closes. Then I whip the hammer out of the bag again and hold it ready.

Now I hear one set of footsteps.

Someone is coming in.

A nervous pulse thumping in my head, I pray that whoever it is does not decide to come into my cubicle. Even if this is one of the hostages, and therefore a potential ally, they could still be dangerous if they scream or cry out or in some other way alert the gunman to my presence. Jamie might not realize it's me before he shoots.

And if it's not Jamie, he won't care anyway.

My hand tightens on the handle of the hammer. I shall hit out first and ask questions later.

My cubicle is the third of five. I hear the person stop and glance into the first cubicle. Then he or she moves on to the second.

Bile rises in my throat and I have to swallow silently. I lift the hammer and hold it ready.

Then the footsteps go into the second cubicle and the door closes and whoever is in there bolts it. I dare not even breathe a sigh of relief, but I take advantage of the noise to climb quietly onto the toilet seat so that no one can see my feet in the gaps under the door and the cubicle divider.

I wait, crouched there on the seat like a hunter

waiting to pounce. But am I really the hunter or am I the prey? I cannot be certain.

There is silence from the cubicle next door. Whoever is in there is much better at peeing silently than I am. But suddenly I hear the soft *thud* of something hitting the floor, and although the noise isn't loud at all, I almost fall off the toilet seat like a dead budgie off a perch.

I just manage to stop myself from toppling over. Then I realize, with a stab of panic, that the unknown person next door has dropped something. Even as I realize this, a large roll of toilet paper appears under the dividing wall. It rolls smoothly towards me, leaving a trail of unravelled paper behind it, and stops at the bottom of the toilet I'm standing on.

I sweat as I strain to keep still, my eyes fixed on the gap under the wall. I see a hand appear, pulling at the toilet roll, trying to reel it back in, and I have to clamp my teeth down on my bottom lip to stop myself from crying out.

For God's sake, leave the bloody loo roll where it is!

The hand continues to pull and simply succeeds in unravelling yet more of the toilet paper. It's a girl's hand, and that is all I can see. Is she a member of Class 9D? Who is she? I long to know, but I can't take that risk.

Unfortunately I might find out anyway in a moment if this idiot decides that, in the middle of an armed siege, it's vital that she steps into the next-door cubicle to retrieve the toilet roll she's just dropped.

I grip the handle of the hammer with cold yet clammy fingers.

The second person, the one who was waiting outside, is now coming in. I hear footsteps. Instantly the girl next door drops the toilet roll again. I hear her rush out of the cubicle, whispering breathless apologies, and then the murmur of their voices as they leave together.

Quickly I climb down from my perch and put my eye to the narrow gap at the side of my half-closed cubicle door, but I can see nothing. The footsteps die away down the corridor, in the direction of 9D's classroom.

That's where I am heading too.

I leave the cubicle and go over to the doorway that leads out into the corridor. I stand there for a moment, assessing my situation. All the blinds on both sides of the annexe are closed, so I am safe and protected from marksmen outside, at least for the moment.

I understand the need for silence though; why those two people were whispering. There could be someone crouched outside on the flat roof right now, their weapon pointed straight at any one of the windows around me, waiting for the slightest noise.

Quiet as a mouse, light as a cat, silent and watchful as a bird of prey, I slip along the corridor towards Class 9D's form room.

Thirteen

All last week the level of tension was building relentlessly inside our house. It was rocketing to the point where just to step through the front door put my nerves on edge and gave me an instant pounding stress headache. My last hope, Leo Jackson, was gone, and there was nothing more I could do. Jamie was in a constant black mood and Mum was still as high as a kite.

There was a sense of imminent danger hanging over me. It was vague and undefined, but it was *there*. And I knew that the threat came from Jamie himself.

By this time I had given up trying to talk Mum into seeing the doctor. In fact, I had given up on *everything*. There was nothing I could do. I could not fight the overwhelming feeling that I was running out of time, that Jamie was already secretly laying his plans. I had no idea what he was going to do but, knowing Jamie as I did, I was very, very afraid. All I could do was wait helplessly.

This was a week of disasters, when emotions boiled up and spilled over, and I finally realized that I was too late, that everything was hurtling out of control and that Jamie would have his way.

It began on Monday when I was rushing to get ready for school. As I was lying awake worrying most of the night instead of sleeping, I was finding it difficult to get up in the mornings. Yawning, cleaning my teeth and trying to strap my watch to my wrist at the same time, I managed to drop the watch into the overflowing bathroom bin.

I swore mildly under my breath as I rooted through used cotton-wool pads and tissues and Mum's half-used, expensive make-up pots. The rubbish would stay there until I got around to emptying it because no one did any housework except me. I found my watch at the bottom of the bin, and there I also found the pregnancy test.

I sat back on my heels, gaping at the white stick in complete disbelief, knowing instantly that Jamie must *not* find out about this.

'Christ! Is that what I think it is?'

Jamie was already there, in the doorway. My heart plunged. I hadn't heard him come up behind me. Jamie's whole body, even his voice, was rigid with fury. If it was possible, he was even angrier than he'd been with Dr Zeelander.

'Jamie, it's negative.' I scrambled hurriedly to my feet, thrusting the stick at him so that he could see for himself. 'She's not pregnant.'

'Maybe not – this time.' Jamie slapped the stick from my hand and it clattered to the floor. 'But what about next time? I am *not* going to let her do this, Mia.'

'It might have been a good thing,' I said weakly. 'If she *was* pregnant, she'd have had to go to the doctor.'

Jamie gave me a look of utter scorn and went out without a word.

By now I had forgotten all about the essay competition. I had written my entry three or four months ago and sealed it in an envelope which I'd given to Ms Kennedy, and she had sent it off. So when I arrived at school that March morning, and Ms Kennedy popped out of the staffroom as I went by, smiling and saying,

'I have a surprise for you today, Mia,' I did not think of the essay competition at all. I didn't have any idea what she was talking about, although I did wonder if perhaps she'd got engaged to her boyfriend. Sharp-suited and handsome as a male model, he occasionally picked her up outside the school gates in his black Porsche.

Stupid me, I didn't even guess when we were sitting in assembly, and Mr Whitman announced that the school had just heard the results of the writing competition.

'I know that several of our students entered this competition, prompted by our head of English, Ms Kennedy,' Mr Whitman said, smiling broadly. 'And so I am absolutely delighted to announce that Mia Jackson of Nine A has won first prize.'

Mr Whitman directed his 100-watt smile, the one he usually reserved for the governors, straight at me, but I swear that at first I thought he meant another Mia Jackson. I wanted to sink straight through the floor as half the school turned to stare at me. The other half probably didn't even know who I was. In fact, I was surprised that Mr Whitman himself was able to pick me out in the crowd.

'Mia, that's fabulous!' Bree whispered warmly in my ear, leaning over to give me a big hug as Ms Kennedy led the applause from the back of the hall. 'Clever you!'

Instantly I turned to Jamie, who was near me, for his approval. He nodded at me and smiled, but he said nothing and there was a look in his eyes that I did not understand.

Just for a moment though, I forgot my problems, I forgot about Mum and not having any money and all the hours spent worrying and wondering about what Jamie might be planning.

Just for that one moment I savoured my victory. Someone somewhere thought that what I had created inside my own head was worthy of a prize. A *first* prize. I had never been first at anything in my whole life. Until then I'd never even felt that I was really part of the human race.

Bree was poking me in the side, and I realized vaguely that Mr Whitman had asked me to go up onto the stage to collect my prize. I stumbled to the front of the hall, which suddenly seemed around two miles long, and shook hands with the headteacher, wishing my fingers didn't feel so sweaty.

I almost snatched my book tokens from Mr Whitman and then scuttled back to my place as fast as I could. I was torn between regret that I hadn't won cash I could use to pay off some of Mum's bills, and avaricious glee that I had a whole one hundred pounds to spend on books. Grandpa had bought me new books occasionally in previous years, but most of what I read had come from the library and gone back there. The thought of going into bookshops and choosing brand-new novels, opening them and smelling the fresh scent of clean white paper, had me gloating like Scrooge over his moneybags.

'And now I'd like to read you Mia's moving and sensitive winning essay called *My Life and the People Most Important to Me*.' Mr Whitman cleared his throat.

Oh, my God.

No.

This was *not* supposed to happen.

I twisted round to look at Ms Kennedy, a dumb,

horrified appeal in my eyes. But she simply gave me an encouraging smile as Mr Whitman read out the words that hadn't been meant for anyone but the judges of the competition to see.

'*When Ms Kennedy came to Hollyfield School to teach us about English literature, everyone could see how beautiful she was. But what I didn't realize then was that Ms Kennedy is just as beautiful inside as she is on the outside . . .*'

I slumped down, my head hanging. I was literally burning with embarrassment, and so hot I thought I might faint. In fact, I wished I *would* faint, and then Mr Whitman would have to stop reading. But I had to sit there, listening to my own words, the words that had looked so meaningful on paper but now sounded shallow and ridiculous. How Ms Kennedy had been so kind to me and had encouraged me to write and had lent me books, and so on and so on and all the rest of it . . .

The essay seemed twice as long as when I originally wrote it. With every word I was willing Mr Whitman to get to the end, and only when he finally did so could

I breathe a little more easily again. There was more applause, and it made me squirm. I wanted to run away and find a paper bag and stick my head in it so that no one could recognize me.

'Oh, Mia,' Bree said, staring at me with a kind of nervous wonder as we all left the hall. 'That was *amazing*. It was *fantastic* . . .'

I felt a little comforted by Bree's words. I had put myself out there, and wasn't that what a real writer would do, regardless of their own embarrassment?

Was I a real writer?

Could I ever be one?

It was a revelation to me, standing there outside the canteen with the smell of cabbage hanging in the air, that a writer was exactly what I wanted to be more than anything in the entire world. I wondered what Jamie would say when I told him.

'Are you a lezzer, Jackson?'

The harsh voice broke into the daydream that had gone from the essay competition to winning the Man Booker Prize in about three seconds.

'What?'

I turned. Bree was trying to pull me away but I was slow to react, still caught up in my fantasy.

Kat Randall stood there, smirking at me, her friends gathered in a half-circle around her. She and I were in different classes and different sets and this was the first time she'd ever spoken to me in three years. I knew about her, though. When we were all in Year Seven she'd been suspended for two weeks for throwing a book at a French teaching assistant.

'You fancy Ms Kennedy, don't you, Jackson?' she said with a dirty laugh as the other girls tittered.

I stared at her. 'Don't be stupid,' I blurted out.

What?!

Get a grip, Mia!

There was simply no way I would ever have said such a thing to anyone like Kat Randall in the past. But I was pleasantly surprised to find that my confidence had instantly and effortlessly soared beyond the stratosphere since finding out I'd won the competition. 'She's been kind to me, that's all.'

'Oh, so that's what they call it these days, is it?' Kat sniggered and her friends all said, '*Oooooooh!*' in high-pitched voices, thick with innuendo, as if they were extras in a *Carry On* film. 'And what about Jamie?' Kat went on. 'Don't you want to tell us more about how much he means to you?'

This time Bree did manage to pull me away, and that was lucky because my new-found fame seemed to have gone straight to my head and I might well have said something that I would later deeply regret. As it was, I didn't worry as much about Kat Randall as I would have done previously. I reasoned that as long as I kept my head down, people at school would have something else to talk about quite soon and I would be forgotten again.

That was my thinking.

You know by now that I am a fool.

But for a day or two I revelled in the new Mia Jackson who had scooped first prize in a writing competition, won one hundred pounds worth of book tokens and now planned to become a writer. I had gone from guaranteed loser to acknowledged winner in one day. I didn't even care when other kids teased me about the essay. I laughed the comments away or simply ignored them. Even Jamie commented on the difference in me.

'Isn't this what I've always told you, Mia?' he challenged me, his dark eyes bright and hopeful for once. '*Now* do you believe me? You can sit back and let life pass you by, or you can step up and grab it with both hands.'

'I know,' I replied. I was brimming with new hope and it was intoxicating, like feeling the warm sun on my face after years in the dark. 'I understand that now, Jamie.'

I was flying high. For once I was able to hold my head up proudly and look at my brother as an equal. I could now imagine a glittering future lying ahead of me, and it seemed easily attainable, just there, almost within my grasp.

'There are only two things that will drag you down.' Jamie's voice held a stark warning. 'One is your own fear. The other is Mum's illness. Just remember that, Mia.'

I didn't reply. In fact, I was hardly listening at all because I stupidly believed that, simply by winning the competition, I had already triumphantly obliterated all traces of the old mouse-like Mia.

I had never felt so confident and so sure of myself.

As for Mum, I decided what was to be done with lightning speed.

Mia Jackson can't make decisions?

You think?

Give me any number of decisions right now, and I'll make them without any hesitation at all.

My intention was to get Mum to the doctor's all on my own, and I had already made the appointment at the surgery. While my plan wasn't foolproof, I thought I could pull it off. I was going to try, anyway. I imagined how amazed and admiring Jamie would be when he found out, and that spurred me on.

I think it was the ancient Greeks who had a word for the way I was feeling then.

Hubris.

It means overweening arrogance, exaggerated pride or self-confidence.

As I'm sure you can guess, my hopes were to come crashing down around my ears.

* * *

'Oh my God, Mia, this is awful.' Mum crumpled the letter in her hand and stared anxiously at me. There were tears in her eyes. You see, despite everything, I know she loves me and because of that, I thought this might work. 'Surely there can't be anything seriously wrong with you, sweetheart?'

The letter was forged, of course, which had been a simple task using one of the computers in the school library. At the top, the school's crest made it look official and I had even copied the real signature of the school nurse at the bottom.

'I don't know, Mum,' I said, sighing a little but not *too* much. I was hoping to give the impression that I was worried, but trying to hide it. I'm no actress, but the confidence I felt after my competition win a few days before was still driving me on. 'I just mentioned to the nurse that I feel tired all the time and my head doesn't feel quite right, and – anyway, she thought our GP should see me for a check-up.'

I was counting heavily on the well-developed sense

of melodrama that was so much a part of Mum's illness, and it did not let me down.

'Oh, Mia.' Mum drew me into her arms. 'I hope there's nothing serious wrong with you, darling. I don't know what I'd do without you – honestly, I really don't.'

'I managed to get a cancellation appointment for this afternoon,' I said. Jamie had vanished straight after school as usual and hadn't come home yet. In fact, he was out more and more at the moment and I'd hardly seen him for the last few days. I was glad about this for once, because it played right into my hands. 'Will you come with me, Mum? I don't want to go alone.'

Mum was still holding me and I felt her stiffen and draw back ever so slightly. She stared down at me and our eyes met, hers wide and horrified, mine innocent and unblinking.

'Oh, Mia, honey . . .' Mum seemed at a loss for words. Tears trembled on her lashes. 'Mia, you know that I—'

'Mum, *please*,' I broke in, trying not to appear as if I was deceiving her, which of course I was. 'I'm getting these terrible headaches and they give me bad dreams, and then my head feels like it's stuffed with cotton wool and I can't think straight. And it's getting worse.' I shivered and buried my face in my hands. 'I didn't want to tell you this, but I'm *really* frightened.'

I peeked at Mum through my fingers. She was looking white and ill herself now. I hated doing this to her, but it was for her own good. I'd played all my cards now. But had I done enough to win the game?

'You don't have to come into the doctor's surgery with me, Mum,' I rushed on. 'You can wait outside in the street, if you like. I don't want to go on my own, just in case . . .'

Mum held me tighter. I could feel her whole body trembling from head to foot, and I knew that she was absolutely terrified, for me and for herself.

'Of course I'll come, darling,' she said shakily. 'And I won't wait in the street – what an idea! I'm coming into the surgery with you.'

'Thanks, Mum.'

We hugged and Mum began to cry silently, her tears dripping onto my hair.

She had reacted exactly as I was hoping she would, but I was careful not to sound too relieved. I was certain that the new, stronger Mia could see this through.

On the journey to the surgery I daydreamed, with immense satisfaction, about what Jamie would say when he eventually came home and discovered that I'd got Mum to the doctor's all by myself.

Then there would be absolutely no need for him to put any of his dark and secret plans, whatever they were, into action, and everything would be all right.

Better than that.

We would all be happy again.

Dr Zeelander had finished her temporary stay at the surgery and left, thank God, and a Dr Richards had now permanently replaced our old GP. I had secretly booked the appointment to see Dr Richards in Mum's name. This was risky, but I didn't want any problems at the surgery like Jamie and I had had with Dr Zeelander. There was a chance that Mum would find out from the receptionist that she was the intended patient before we even went in to see the doctor. She would undoubtedly find out when the doctor called her in. I figured, though, that if Mum threw one of her legendary tantrums at the surgery, that would be enough. Surely the doctors would do something for her then.

But when we went into the clinically clean, white-painted waiting room, luck was on my side, for once.

'I'll just tell the receptionist I'm here for my appointment,' I murmured.

Mum nodded, and to my delight and relief she went straight over to the window and sat there, her back to all the sniffling, wheezing patients, staring out at the traffic rushing past. She looked stiff and straight and uncomfortable, as if she couldn't wait to get out of there.

I waited by the desk in an agony of impatience for the receptionist to finish her telephone conversation and then said in the lowest voice I could get away with: 'Mrs Annabel Jackson, four forty-five p.m.'

The receptionist nodded. 'Take a seat, please.'

I sat down next to Mum. She didn't say anything but she gripped my fingers tightly with a cold, clammy hand. I could see beads of sweat on her forehead.

I didn't know if she was worried for me or for herself. Both, I guessed. Her phobia about doctors and hospitals and medicine was puzzling because it was so all-consuming.

'Mrs Jackson?' The receptionist had one phone in her hand, the receiver covered, and another was ringing next to her. She looked harassed. 'I'm afraid Doctor Richards has been delayed returning from a meeting. Will you be able to wait till five o'clock for your appointment?'

Everything seemed to happen in slow motion. I turned to look at Mum. She glanced at me and then at the receptionist.

'*My* appointment?' she repeated, quite pleasantly.

'Yes, I'm so sorry,' the receptionist replied, 'but Doctor Richards won't be able to see you until five.'

Mum's eyes met mine. I tried to bluff it out, to hold my nerve, but I found I could not fight years of conditioning. My reserves of newly discovered confidence turned out to be as shallow as a puddle. They drained away as swiftly as if someone had pulled out the plug, and my eyes fell.

Mum did not cause a scene, my very last hope. She rose to her feet.

'Unfortunately I can't wait,' she said quietly. She even smiled.

'Maybe you'd like to make another appointment—' the receptionist began, but Mum was out of there like a bat out of hell before she'd even finished the sentence.

I rushed after her. She was already running off down the street.

'Mum! *Mum!*'

I caught up with her outside the Spar minimarket only because the heel had come off one of her ridiculous and expensive stiletto shoes.

'How dare you, Mia!' Raging, Mum turned on me, to the bewilderment of the people waiting at the bus stop outside the parade of shops. 'How *dare* you make a doctor's appointment for me? How dare you *presume*—?'

Her anger was so great, she couldn't spit the words out fast enough as she tried to hobble away from me. 'I'm not a *child*, Mia! Stop interfering in my life!'

'Mum, can we go home and talk about this?'

I pleaded in an undertone, attempting to take her arm. The force of her fury was frightening, just like Jamie's, in fact. 'I didn't mean—'

'*Of course you meant it!*' Mum shrieked. 'Be honest about that at least. You lied to me and tricked me into thinking you might be seriously ill, for God's sake!' She pulled off her heel-less shoe and threw it at me, and everyone in the bus queue instinctively ducked. 'Keep away from me!'

She limped off. I chased after her, knowing that I was slipping inexorably down the slippery slope to misery again, the cold, dark place that I thought I had escaped from for ever just a few days before.

Stupid, stupid, stupid Mia.

'Mum, you need help,' I gasped through tears.

'Leave me alone, Mia,' Mum shouted.

She shoved me aside, kicked off her other shoe and ran, vanishing down the street in bare feet.

I had failed. And why should I be surprised? Because I *am* a failure. I'd just temporarily forgotten the truth in all the heady euphoria of winning the competition.

This is my life and this is who I am and there is nothing I can do to change things.

Beaten and dispirited, I dragged myself home. Mum was ranting and screaming in the living room, occasionally throwing ornaments at the wall. Jamie was there, and he and I stood in the doorway watching her but keeping well out of the way.

'It's my fault,' I whispered. 'I almost managed to get her to see the doctor.'

'Well, you tried,' Jamie muttered. He did not look at me. His eyes were fixed on Mum.

'Stop whispering!' Mum shrieked, turning on us. 'You're always talking, talking, talking behind my back – you're doing my head in! I'm telling you now for the last time, stop interfering! I am *not* going to the doctor's!' She advanced on us, her long corkscrew curls flying, eyes blazing. She looked beautiful but terrifying, like some ancient, snake-haired goddess. 'I am not going to the doctor's now or ever! *Ever!* Do you understand?'

'Yes, Mum,' I replied, defeated.

Jamie did not say anything. He turned to look at

me, and the expression in his eyes was resigned yet determined, and I was so afraid, I could not breathe. I watched as he closed the living-room door very quietly on Mum.

I knew that time had run out.

This was the end, and he and I both knew it.

We stood there in the hall, Jamie calm and controlled, me shaking and petrified.

'Tell me, Jamie!' I gasped. I was almost hysterical and I didn't care if he saw it. 'Tell me what you're going to do.'

'I think we have to make Mum realize what she stands to lose if she doesn't do what she knows she has to,' Jamie replied in a measured voice. 'That is, go to the doctor herself and get help of her own free will.'

'*Lose?*' My voice was a harsh croak. 'What do you mean, Jamie?'

Jamie moved away from me, over to the front door.

'We push Mum to the edge,' he said tightly. 'Just like she's done to us so many times. We make her see that she can't go on like this, that she can't have everything just the way she wants it. We make her sit up and take notice of us, once and for all.'

'How?' I cried wildly. 'I don't know what you mean. Jamie, you're scaring me!'

'It's the only way, Mia,' Jamie said softly.

He would not say a word more. All I knew was that something terrible, something earth-shattering, was going to happen, and there was nothing I could do to stop it.

Mum crept into bed with me later that night and hugged me and cried and said she was sorry. But it was too late. The new Mia, the Mia who had briefly been my friend and had promised so much, had gone. She had vanished into the night, and I did not think she would ever come again.

I had no strength left now, for anything. I could not force Jamie to share his secrets with me and I didn't even try. I found it impossible now to laugh away or shrug off the sarcastic comments and rude sniggers about that bloody essay.

And I did not even try to protect myself against the taunts of Kat Randall, who had been in the Spar minimarket the night before and had witnessed everything.

'So, tell me, how *is* your mum today, Mia?'

Smug, gleeful, gloating Kat was waiting for me at the school gates the next morning. She must have made sure she arrived early just to taunt me, because her late marks were legendary in number.

'Have to say, she looked as mad as a box of frogs when I saw you both yesterday,' Kat went on, staring at me intently so that she could enjoy my pain and humiliation to the full. 'God, that was embarrassing when she threw her shoe at you, wasn't it?'

And so Kat Randall began her campaign of harassment, one that looked set to run and run, possibly for the next few years. It's almost laughable that my life should become euphoric so very briefly and then plunge into even blacker misery, all in the space of a few days.

There was nothing I could do about it, even if I wanted to. The old Mia was back with a vengeance, and all I could do was wait and watch, helpless as a new-born, to see what Jamie would do.

I trembled with fear for Jamie, for Mum and for myself.

I did not know where it would all end.

Now I know.

Here, in school.

With a gun.

Fourteen

Monday 10 March, 10.03 a.m.

I know that Jamie is near.

Our old telepathy isn't failing me.

Or is it just my imagination?

As I tiptoe down the corridor, there is a tingling in my fingertips, my heart beats faster and I can almost hear Jamie breathing in my ear.

'Talk to me, Jamie,' I murmur. 'Where are you?'

And I listen for his voice, but there is no one speaking inside my head except myself.

I am so close and yet still so far. I want to run down the corridor to Class 9D's form room as fast as I can, burst in and get this nerve-shredding situation over once and for all. But I restrain myself.

Patience, Mia.

Running would be reckless and I can't risk alerting

anyone inside that classroom, friend or enemy, to my presence. Not until I have worked out how the hell I'm going to let Jamie know that I am not an armed police officer.

Is Jamie waiting for me?

Does he know or has he guessed that I will come?

Surely he can sense that I am close by, like I can sense him?

I wonder, with a surge of fear like a jolt of electricity, if Jamie will listen to me at all.

Will he stop and abandon this just because I ask him to?

I don't know.

Maybe I'm in just as much danger, whether the gunman is Jamie or a stranger. Either way, I may end up fighting for my life. But still I continue on my way with slow, silent steps.

Like the main school building, the annexe has been extended and built onto over the years, and it is a warren of twisting corridors, a rat-run with lots of hiding places.

I imagine Jamie watching and waiting, wondering

who will be the next person to walk through the classroom door. Somehow I have to let him know that I am here or take a chance that might prove dangerous, possibly fatal. I can't rely on our telepathic link, it is far too fragile and insubstantial if it even exists at all now. And I can't charge in, all guns blazing – excuse the pun. I can't open the classroom door until I'm sure that Jamie won't attack me straight away, not realizing who I am.

I have to make it out of here, otherwise who will look after Mum?

Leo Jackson?

What a joke.

I push the thought of my father away. I don't need any useless emotion right now. I don't know why his name came to mind, anyway.

I could call out and Jamie would recognize my voice. But that could be even more dangerous if it is *not* Jamie. I must not lose sight of the fact that it is possible, maybe even more logical, that it's someone else.

Either way, I could be the one who suffers unless I keep my wits about me.

I could write a note and slide it under the door, I think.

The idea is so absurd, I almost laugh aloud. But it's the best one I have at this moment.

The silence in the corridor roars in my ears. I had never realized before that complete silence could sound so loud or be so terrifying. Every breath I take, every beat of my heart, every creak of my joints seems to resonate loudly, booming in the still, dusty air.

The corridor, shrouded in blinds, is gloomy and getting gloomier. I guess that, outside, the sun has slipped out of sight behind clouds and the sky is turning grey. The temperature has dropped a few degrees and I shiver. I am cold, but it's also because I am afraid.

Strangely, thoughts of giving up do not enter my head.

I stop. I have not forgotten that when I step round this corner, 9D's form room will be straight ahead of me.

I must be ready.

I press myself against the wall and take one quick,

controlled look round the corner and down the corridor.

There is the classroom, the white-painted door standing out like a beacon in the dim light.

What is happening behind it?

Is Jamie really there?

Is he standing, with a gun, in front of Class 9D?

Menacing them, threatening them?

Even now that I am actually here, it still seems so totally unbelievable.

I cannot help wondering if I have made a huge mistake.

But I feel even more strongly now that Jamie is near me.

The door blind is pulled down so I can't see inside, but more importantly, no one can see out either. There is not a single sound to be heard.

I wonder how many weapons are trained on this very room from the outside.

Flattening myself against the wall of the corridor, I begin to slide my way along to that door. My primeval instinct is to shut off every function of my body that might make a noise, and that includes breathing, but I realize that if I do that, I will pass out. Not a good idea. Instead I inhale and exhale rhythmically, attempting to keep my heartbeat regular and measured.

I fail.

I reach the door. Still I can hear nothing. Beads of sweat roll down my cheeks; all my senses are on high alert. Is there anyone inside? Or have they moved elsewhere? And if Mrs Lucas, Class 9D and Jamie *are* in the classroom, then why aren't they making any noise?

I fear the worst and a whimper of fear almost escapes me, but I clamp my teeth down on my bottom lip and keep quiet. Then I sink to my knees and slowly, gracefully, without touching either the door or the wooden surround, I lean forward and peer through the keyhole.

I see – nothing. Only darkness.

I grit my teeth as I realize that either the key is in the lock on the other side of the door, or someone has deliberately blocked the keyhole. I want to scream with frustration, but of course I don't.

What now? I yell inside my head. *For God's sake, Mia, what now?*

Even as I'm thinking this, my gaze falls on the cupboard next door. This cupboard is where French textbooks are kept, and inside it has a connecting door that opens into the back of class 9D's form room. I remember this from my Year Eight French lessons.

I have to make a supreme effort not to fling the cupboard door open and rush straight inside. Instead I reach for the handle and ease it down. For a second it doesn't move and I think it's locked. But a little extra pressure, and the door clicks open.

I slip into the cupboard. I have to shut the door gently behind me – it might arouse suspicion if I leave it open. But there is no window inside the cupboard and it is so dark in there, I can't see anything. There's a light switch, but I dare not use it. However, I can work out where the connecting door should be from my knowledge of the classroom. Feeling my way past the bookshelves, I head in that direction, praying I do not knock any copies of *Madame Bovary* or *Bonjour,*

Madame! A First Course in French for Beginners to the floor.

My memory does not fail me. As I move further forward, I see a sliver of light ahead of me. It is shining under the connecting door; a tiny beam shows me where the keyhole is.

Once again I kneel, and once again I do not touch the door or the surround. My heart is thundering as I lean forward and delicately place my eye to the keyhole.

This time I *can* see into Class 9D's form room.

I only have a narrow angle of vision, but there are people in front of me, sitting at tables. They seem alive, moving ever so slightly as I watch, and relief rips through me. I can't see Kat Randall, but I can just glimpse Mrs Lucas at her desk. I can't see her face though because her head is bowed.

I swivel my head a little more, trying to see all corners of the room, but the keyhole is too small. I cannot see Jamie. Or anyone with a gun for that matter.

I straighten up. I wonder what to do now; I can only think of one plan. I could go out into the corridor, make some noise or other to draw the hostage-taker out of the classroom, and then hide.

When I know whether it is Jamie or not, then I'll decide what to do.

Bree's words come back to me, and I hope he isn't wearing a mask because I don't have a back-up plan.

This is my only hope, I think.

I turn to leave the cupboard as silently as I came. That was my intention, anyway. But as I begin to feel my way back towards the other door, the plastic bag looped through my belt cannot cope with the weight of the hammer any longer.

The handles tear right through, but in the dark I do not see.

I don't realize until the hammer clatters to the floor with a crash that seems to reverberate through the whole of the silent annexe.

Fifteen

Monday 10 March, 10.10 a.m.

I have put my plan into action a little earlier than I expected.

As screams echo in the classroom next door, I blunder and stumble through the darkness of the cupboard, back towards the other door. Books go flying as I bump into the shelves, trying to feel my way out.

I reach the door and grab the handle and it sticks again. Gulping for air, sobbing, gasping, I push down on it – hard – and the door flies open.

As I hurtle out of the cupboard, I hear the unmistakable sound of someone fumbling to unlock the classroom door. The screams and shouts are suddenly silenced.

'Oh, God! Oh, *God*!'

I run faster than I've ever run before. I am literally running for my life. My nose is running, my eyes are wet, my breath is rasping in my chest. I dare not look back to see what is happening behind me. *I have to get to the corner before I'm seen, before I become a target, a sitting duck* . . .

My muscles burn as, legs and arms pumping, I finally round the corner. As I do so, I hear the classroom door being flung open. There's a short delay, and then I hear the sound of heavy footsteps running in my direction.

Someone is coming for me.

I guess it has to be the person with the gun. But surely he wouldn't have left his hostages unguarded? He must have some other method of keeping them under control.

It *cannot* be anyone else.

This is him, and he's coming after me.

He is only a few metres away, round the corner.

Curiously, the prospect of imminent danger – maybe even death – calms me. It's as if a switch has been flipped in my brain and, robot-like, I am immediately thrown into ice-cool mode.

This is my chance to find out if it's Jamie or not.

I have to be somewhere, hidden, where I can *see*. And before I put myself in any more danger, if that is at all possible.

The footsteps come closer. I run silently, balancing on my toes like a dancer, into a nearby classroom and duck behind the door, leaving it ajar. I press myself into the shadows and put my eye to the narrow gap next to the door hinges. The classroom is dim, and so is the corridor outside, but I am sure I will recognize Jamie, whatever happens.

I will *know*. I will *feel* that he is here.

Someone comes round the corner. He has slowed down now and is moving cautiously, making hardly a sound except for soft, calculated footsteps. But the angle of his approach is such that, frustratingly, I cannot see who it is through the very small space between door and frame.

I hear the door of the classroom next to mine open. A moment later, the one opposite.

He is checking all the classrooms.

Suddenly the door I am hiding behind is pushed

open a little further. I almost collapse onto my knees, but somehow I find the backbone to stay upright and as still and as silent as I can. Only the door, one thin piece of wood, separates us now, and on the other side I can hear someone breathing, shallow and panicky, in time with me.

Jamie, it's me, I say silently inside my head, willing the telepathy we had to come to my aid now, when I need it most.

Jamie is here, I'm sure of it. I feel it so strongly that the hair on the back of my neck stands up and makes me shiver.

It *must* be him on the other side of this door.

But my overwhelming fear keeps me wary, and I stay hidden. I had to leave the hammer behind in the dark cupboard in my rush to escape, and so I am now unarmed. I can't take the ultimate risk of trusting my instincts and my senses. I have to see for myself.

He's leaving . . .

I hear him creep along the corridor. He is going further away from the classroom, into the rest of the first floor of the annexe.

He is searching for me.

Quickly I put my eye to the gap again, twisting my head, trying to get a look at the mystery person. As he pushed the door open further, so the narrow space widened.

I catch a glimpse of someone dressed in black just before he edges his way round the corner of the corridor. I see he is carrying a blue rucksack on his back.

I also see the black gun in his hand. It is not Grandpa's gun.

My God.

It is not Jamie.

Sixteen

Monday 10 March, 10.17 a.m.

Outside the sun drifts out from behind the clouds and peers round the edges of the blinds, lighting up the corridors and classrooms a little. I stay where I am behind the door because my legs will not move. I am shaking uncontrollably. Nausea threatens to overcome me and I clap my hand silently over my mouth, willing myself not to retch.

The gunman is not Jamie.

And now, for the very first time, I realize exactly how much danger I am in.

The figure in black is a little shorter and much stockier than Jamie. He is not my brother, I'm certain of that.

And yet I'm also certain that Jamie is in the annexe. He's close by, he is here *somewhere*.

So what has happened to him?

Where *is* he?

A sob rises in my throat and I press the back of my hand against my mouth to stifle it.

Now I'm faced with a different, but no less difficult decision. Do I go back and attempt to help the hostages, or do I try to get the hell out of here?

I remember that at least two sets of doors on the ground floor of the annexe are locked. Could they *all* be locked?

If so, I can't get out anyway.

And besides, I don't *want* to leave until I find out what has happened to Jamie.

I rest my head against the door, my mind a maelstrom of confusing, racing thoughts: *Jamie, Class 9D, Mrs Lucas, the police watching and waiting outside . . .*

What is the best way for me to help them all, and to help myself too?

I make a decision.

I step out of the classroom and glide silently after the figure in black.

Am I crazy?

Possibly.

I have no thought in my head except the vague idea that I might somehow trap him somewhere.

Don't ask me how.

When I reach the next corner, I stop abruptly, pressing myself against the wall, wondering if I dare look. I hope he cannot hear my heart thudding and pounding against my chest.

Imagine if he's waiting for me on the other side of this corner, I think, my skin crawling. Imagine if I look and he's standing there, pointing the gun at me.

I wait a few more seconds, but I know I have to take a chance. I have no choice.

So I go for it and stick my head round the wall like a nervous tortoise.

Relief.

There is no one there.

But as I am about to step out and move on, I see a shadow in the doorway of the science lab, spotlit by the sunbeams dancing their way past the sides of the blinds.

That is *his* shadow.

He's still searching for me.

Instantly I pull myself back out of sight before the shadow becomes reality and he steps out into the corridor again. But as I do so, I notice a sudden, quicksilver flash of bright light.

The sunbeams are glinting on the shiny metal of the gun, reflecting off it.

I wait.

I wait and I calculate how much time it will take him to search the rooms on this stretch of corridor.

I wonder if he will give up and return to the classroom. If he does, the shortest way is back round this corner where I am standing.

And what then?

If he doesn't come back this way, if he goes on and continues to search for me, then he will come to the very centre of the annexe. There the corridor widens out into a large square landing with an ironwork balcony that overlooks the main entrance, down on the ground floor.

The landing is huge and wood-panelled; it is open and exposed and there is nowhere to hide. There is only one door leading off it, and that leads into the school's careers centre.

I hear another door open. I calculate that this is the last room he will be checking before he turns another corner and reaches the wide, open space of the landing.

If I'm going to follow him, and it looks as if that is exactly what I am going to do despite my common sense telling me otherwise, I have to give him enough time to search the careers centre and then move on into the other part of the annexe. I can't risk being caught on the landing. There I will be trapped like a rabbit in headlights, with nowhere to run to.

I bite my lip hard enough to draw blood, and the pain spurs me on. Running lightly and quietly, I clear the last length of corridor in a few seconds. Then I wait at the next corner.

Even now he must be crossing the landing, and there is nowhere to search except the careers centre where dowdy, bespectacled and terminally gloomy Miss Walters sits day after day, trying to persuade pupils that they really *don't* want to be the next David

Beckham, Lewis Hamilton or Lindsay Lohan. She urges them to become teachers or doctors or nurses or to get a job in IT or the civil service. Bree always used to say that Miss Walters couldn't possibly have any influence on anyone, since she herself had obviously been dumb enough to choose a career she thoroughly disliked.

Poor Bree.

She must be wondering what the hell is happening to me, especially if Ms Powell has informed the police that I am still inside. And she *must* have done. Everyone knows by now, I'm sure.

I wonder if someone has told Mum.

Everything that has happened, like seeing the TV report and Ms Kennedy's accident, seems a thousand years ago, and I am shocked when I glance at my watch to see that only a little over an hour has passed since the school was evacuated.

I peer round the corner.

I can see the landing where the corridor widens out and becomes square. Sunshine is still sneaking in around the blinds, lighting up the open space, and dust motes float lazily in the air.

212

On the left-hand side of the landing I can see the door of the careers centre. It is closed.

On the right side I can see the long, curving metal balcony above the ground floor.

Once I am out on the landing, I am naked, unarmed and vulnerable.

My fear is intense. It makes me gasp and gulp for air as if I am having a panic attack, and desperately I try to calm myself as I pull back out of sight again.

Once more I wait, pressed against the wall, my whole body one mass of intense, quivering nerves. Surely he can't *still* be searching the careers centre. There are hardly any hiding places among Miss Walters' obsessively neat shelves of university handbooks and careers leaflets.

But I wait three more long, stomach-churning minutes, just to be certain.

And still he does not come out.

I now know that he has gone on into the other part of the annexe and I am safe to go after him.

Well, I am safe as long as he doesn't suddenly decide to come back this way again.

I don't want to think about that.

I step out round the corner and run for it. As I cross the landing, past the door of the careers centre, I glance over the balcony at the ground floor below. I wonder if the police are waiting somewhere near the entrance, waiting and watching for their chance to burst in.

Somewhere in the maze of corridors on the other side of the annexe, I will trap him, and then I will return to 9D's classroom.

Because I am not leaving without finding out what has happened to Jamie.

A sudden quicksilver glint of light flashes in my eyeline. It pulls me up short, my heart jumping, my guts turning to water. I see that the door of the careers centre is opening, very, very slowly.

He can't have been searching the careers centre all this time. He has been lying in wait for me. He has been playing with me like a cat plays with a mouse. He has heard my footsteps and now he's closing in for the kill.

There is nowhere to hide.

Wait.

There *is* one way I can go.

Swiftly, silently, I climb up onto the metal handrail of the balcony. I do not allow myself even a second to look down at the ground floor so far below me.

Instead I swing myself over the rail and into space.

Seventeen

Monday 10 March, 10.23 a.m.

I hang off the balcony, my body suspended in mid-air. I am gripping two of the iron railings right at the bottom, one in each hand, like grim death. The metal is ice-cold and smooth to the touch. Too smooth. I am worried that my fingers will simply slide off, however tightly I hold on. My hands are the only things keeping me up, the only supports preventing me from falling to the ground floor and breaking bones.

The sunlight has vanished again and grey dimness surrounds me. I hear soft footfalls as he comes stealthily out of the careers centre. He thought he had trapped me and now *he's* wondering where *I* have gone. My arms are already feeling the strain of bearing my whole weight, and muscles and sinews are stretching too far and beginning to ache and burn.

I have to fight my natural instinct, which is to allow my legs to flail back and forth in the air around me. Instead, I hang perfectly straight and still, metres above the ground floor, not moving – as far as I am able. I am reminded of a movie Jamie and I watched together in which someone was hanged for a crime he did not commit. I imagine hanging, dead, and make all my limbs go limp.

The only parts of me that are still at all visible are my hands, gripping the railings. I can only hope that he doesn't glance down and see them. I cannot see him at all. I won't be able to see him unless he comes to the balcony and peers over the edge. The gloom that has now descended on the annexe again gives me courage.

He stops in the middle of the landing.

I hang there in suspense, literally.

Then, after what seems like an hour or two, he leaves. I close my eyes briefly, not even daring to breathe a sigh of relief.

I can tell from the sound of his steps that he is slowly going back in the direction of 9D's classroom.

By this time my arms have almost dislocated

themselves from their sockets. Giving silent thanks that I am skinny and underweight, I silently begin to swing and flail and thrash about until, panting, I manage to lift one leg and get a tenuous toe-hold on the edge of the balcony. I make an enormous effort, hook my foot between the railings and then haul myself up, falling clumsily over the handrail. I am shaking, not with relief, but with the adrenalin that is now screaming through my veins.

'Now it's my turn,' I say to myself.

I am exhilarated because he thought he had outwitted me, but instead I have fooled him.

We're still playing the cat-and-mouse game. But this time, I'm the cat.

Call me crazy, but I go charging after him.

And as I run, I do two things.

First, I set the alarm on my watch to go off in one minute. Second, I pull my tie from my pocket and make a noose at one end of it.

Then I speed up. I can only be a few seconds behind him now. He must be just round the next corner, on his way back to 9D's form room.

Twenty seconds before my watch alarm goes off.

I laid my plans and chose the site for my trap carefully, while I was hanging off the balcony in mid-air moments earlier. I race into one of the Year Eight classrooms and there I place my watch on the teacher's desk. Then I dash out again and across the corridor into the science lab opposite. I duck behind the door out of sight.

'Five – four – three – two – one,' I whisper.

My alarm begins to beep. It sounds eerily loud and tinny in the silent building.

He comes running back almost immediately.

Christ, I never realized I was so close behind him!

He was literally a metre away, just round the corner.

This time there is no attempt at silence because he thinks he has me.

The truth is that I now have *him*.

I hear him hurtle into the classroom. Instantly I am out of the science lab, tie in hand.

I whip the classroom door shut, loop the noose over the door handle and tighten it with shaking fingers.

Dropping to my knees, I begin to wind the other end of the tie around the valve of the radiator that sits conveniently close to the classroom door.

Suddenly there is a blood-curdling scream of rage. Then someone is pulling violently at the door from inside the room, almost tugging the remaining length of my tie from my grasp. My insides are turning to water; I sob and pant with fear as I knot the tie firmly in place.

The door is now tethered tightly shut. *I hope.*

Slowly, fearfully, I stand up. I let out an ear-splitting scream myself as I see a face pressed against the glass in the top of the door.

Christ. It is Lee Curtis.

Lee Curtis, Year Ten student, drug dealer and Kat Randall's ex-boyfriend.

Lee is banging on the glass with the gun and yelling, his eyeballs bulging, his face red and contorted with unbelievable fury. He catches sight of me then, and he stops shouting momentarily. Even though I want to, I can't move and I can't drag my eyes away from him.

Lee looks stupefied, utterly dumbfounded. It seems

to take him a few seconds to realize that it's me, Mia Jackson, who has got the better of him.

'Let me out, you stupid bitch!' he snarls.

'I have some bad news for you, Lee!' I yell, suddenly exhilarated beyond measure, even though tears are pouring down my cheeks. 'I'm not going to be bullied by you or anyone else ever again!'

Lee lets out another animal roar of fury. I can see him through the glass, struggling to throw off his rucksack as he kicks savagely at the door handle.

A thrill of horror runs through me. *I have to get help right now before Lee shoots his way out and comes after me.*

'Jamie!' I shriek, my voice hoarse as I spin round and race off down the corridor. My intention is to get down to the ground floor, smash a window and alert the police. 'I know you're here, Jamie. *Where are you?*'

Then there is a white-hot flash and it's accompanied by the loudest bang I have ever heard. The classroom door blows off its hinges and there is a sound of breaking glass and the force of the blast sends me flying head-first down the corridor. There is smoke, people are screaming, my ears are ringing and I have no idea what is happening.

I crash heavily to the ground.

I see stars and then I black out.

Eighteen

Monday 10 March, 2.10 p.m.

I can see stars.

I am floating through darkness. Every so often a silver star shimmers in the gloom. But when I put out my hand to touch it, it always eludes me, shooting away and leaving a trail of flame in its wake.

I feel weightless and relaxed.

I am happy.

But now I am being pulled roughly in the opposite direction. I try to fight it, but the force is too strong for me.

'*No!*' I shout.

I am hurtling through time and space towards a light so bright it is burning me up. I don't want to go there, but I have no choice. The lovely feeling of weightlessness vanishes, and now my body becomes heavy and bruised and battered.

I try to speak, but I can't. My eyelids flutter and open very slowly.

At first I see only pure, clean white, and I think I'm lying on a cloud. Then I realize that I am in a small white-painted room, in a bed covered with snowy linen. The light is even brighter now, and my eyes begin to water painfully. A sob rises in my throat and I squeeze my eyes shut.

'Mia?'

I recognize the soft voice at my ear. It's Mum. With an effort, I open my eyes a little again and turn my head. But Mum is just an outline, a misty blur.

'Oh, thank God,' Mum murmurs, and starts to cry.

I see more outlines in the room, outlines that gradually begin to take shape. I make out a woman in uniform and a man in a white coat. I am so disorientated, it takes me a little while to work out that I am in hospital.

Why?

I struggle to remember what happened. My brain

seems to be working at a much slower rate than the rest of me, and I cannot make any logical sense of the dark, senseless, tangled mess that is my mind.

But I know there is something I need to ask.

I try to swallow, but it takes ages.

'Jamie?' I whisper.

I speak so low, no one can hear me. My voice isn't right. It's cracked and harsh and it sounds like someone else speaking.

'What did you say, darling?'

Mum leans over me and her face swims into focus a little more. She takes my hand. The doctor comes closer too, and so does the nurse.

I lick my dry lips, wishing I did not feel as if a vat of thick treacle had been poured into my brain, slowing down every thought process.

'Jamie.' This time I manage to raise my voice just a little. 'Jamie. Where is he? I couldn't find him.'

Mum gasps. She looks uncertainly at me, and then at the doctor. Tears begin to roll down her face, although she does not make a sound.

'Has something happened to Jamie?' I am desperate

to make them understand my need for answers. 'I have to know!'

The doctor leans over me. He is middle-aged and grey-haired.

'How are you feeling, Mia?' he asks.

I ignore him. 'Where's Jamie?' I repeat.

And then, too late, I realize what I'm saying.

Even in my confused and dazed state, I know that I have made a huge mistake.

The doctor frowns. 'Mia,' he says gently. 'Tell me. Who is Jamie?'

Nineteen

'I *have told you something about the people who mean a lot to me – my teacher Ms Kennedy, my best friend Bree and my grandfather*,' Dr Macdonald reads aloud in an expressionless voice. '*But no one is more important in my life than my twin brother Jamie, who died when I was born.*'

Dr Macdonald lays the pages of my prize-winning essay on her desk and looks at me. She is petite and her black hair is as shiny as a TV shampoo ad. She wears it in a French pleat to show off her long neck. Her knee-length shift dress is fitted and chic and navy blue in colour; her court shoes match exactly. She's a psychologist or a psychiatrist, I can never remember the difference. A head doctor, anyway.

I'm still in hospital although physically I am well again. For the past few weeks I've been having sessions with Dr Macdonald; eventually, to my surprise, I want to talk. At first I was suspicious of her, but now my emotional dam has cracked open and words pour out of me like a waterfall. I am the human equivalent of Niagara Falls. I don't care what anyone thinks of me any more. I seem to have grown a tougher, harder shell around my previously touch-sensitive skin. I tell Dr Macdonald about Mum and Grandpa, about Michael Riley and Caroline Zeelander and Leo Jackson and all the others.

I tell her everything and hold back nothing.

Dr Macdonald listens, but rarely interrupts during those first sessions. Her smooth, oval, fine-featured face shows no signs of either incredulity or condemnation. Or sympathy, for that matter. Her expression is of polite but intense interest, for the most part, and gives me no clue to what she is thinking.

'I want you to know that there's nothing wrong with me,' I say calmly. 'My mind is as clear as crystal and as sound as a bell. I've known all the time that Jamie doesn't exist as you or I do. That when he was born, he was already dead. I've always known that he's a ghost.'

Wait, that's not quite true. When we were very young, I didn't know. From my very earliest memories, Jamie was just *there*, my twin and constant companion. Mum and Grandpa and my nursery teachers and everyone else played along when I insisted that Jamie got the things I did – birthday cards and birthday balloons and sweets and all the rest of it.

After all, it's cute, isn't it, that a four-year-old has an imaginary friend?

It was only gradually, when I saw the sidelong glances and the frowns of disapproval on people's faces, that I realized a seven-year-old with an invisible companion is not acceptable.

And so I learned to keep quiet. But Jamie was still there, a solid, real presence in my life. When I wrote about him in my prize-winning essay, I was very careful not to give away my secret.

My brother is always with me. I feel him around me. He watches over me like a guardian angel, and I always know when he is near . . .

But I did not say anywhere in that essay that I *see* Jamie and talk to him and he talks to me. Because I

231

know people won't understand, and even people who *say* they believe in ghosts will think I'm crazy.

'Do *you* believe in ghosts?' I ask Dr Macdonald.

Dr Macdonald has a way of thinking things through for a moment or two before replying, as if she is afraid she might incriminate herself by saying the wrong thing. Her pale brow furrows slightly and she brushes a stray hair neatly back into her French pleat.

'I don't believe the case has been sufficiently proven yet, by any means,' she says.

'*I* believe in them,' I say boldly. 'You might think I'm not quite right in the head, but I'm not the only one. Lots of people think that ghosts exist.'

'But not many of them live with a ghost on a daily basis,' Dr Macdonald replies gently.

I am silent. She's right, of course.

'You don't believe Jamie is a ghost,' I say. 'You think I'm seeing things.'

This time Dr Macdonald doesn't answer my question. Our conversation appears to be a kind of game. We're playing cat and mouse, rather like Lee Curtis and I did in the annexe, but with words this time. I think Dr Macdonald sees herself very much as the cat, but I'm not ready to roll over and die just yet.

'Is Jamie here now?' she asks.

My smile vanishes. 'No. I haven't seen him since that morning.'

The last time I saw Jamie was when he was on his way to the annexe. This is the longest time since we were babies that we haven't been together, and it feels like I've lost half of myself.

Why doesn't he come?

'Do you know anything of the circumstances of your birth, Mia?' Dr Macdonald asks, changing the subject yet again. Another of her tactics. 'Yours and Jamie's?'

I shake my head.

'Apparently it was a difficult one, and there were complications,' she explains gently. 'Your mother was attended by a relatively inexperienced doctor, and all these factors affected what happened to Jamie.'

I bite my lip, feeling deep, profound sadness. I am now beginning to understand Mum's pathological dislike of doctors and hospitals.

'Does . . .' I swallow. 'Did Mum realize that my "imaginary" childhood friend was my brother?'

I choke a little on the words. I can imagine all too vividly the pain this would have caused Mum and I regret it bitterly, even though I was too young to know at the time.

'I believe she suspected it, although she was never sure,' Dr Macdonald replies. 'Apparently she read some research that indicated twins retain memories of each other from the womb, even when one of them dies before or during birth.'

'Mum told you all this?' I ask hesitantly.

'Yes.' Dr Macdonald holds my gaze. 'Does that surprise you, Mia?'

'A little,' I admit. 'I guess it's taken something pretty drastic to force Mum to talk about it. Like me being involved in an armed siege.'

'This is what you thought would happen, though, isn't it?' Dr Macdonald remarks.

I stare uncomprehendingly at her.

'You told me earlier,' she goes on, 'how you felt you had to push your mother into getting medical help by making her sit up and take notice of you.'

'Oh,' I say, suddenly understanding. 'That wasn't me. It was Jamie.'

'Yes.' Dr Macdonald's face is a smooth, expressionless mask. 'Well, we shall make sure your mother gets the help she needs this time, Mia. Don't worry about that. Now, I think our time is up for today.'

I am grateful to Dr Macdonald, but that doesn't stop me from clinging tenaciously to what I damn well *know*. That Jamie has been with me all these years, and that he is a ghost.

A *real* ghost.

I think that's probably an oxymoron.

No one seems to know exactly why Lee Curtis did what he did, or what he was expecting to happen as a result. He had a grudge against the school, and particularly against Mrs Lucas, as she was the teacher who had caught him dealing and got him suspended. And maybe he was showing off for Kat Randall's benefit too.

But the gun Lee was carrying was only a replica,

bought on the internet. More sinister were the explosive devices he had brought into school, hidden in his rucksack. Again, these had been prepared following instructions he had found online. Lee placed these devices around 9D's classroom, then attaching one to the door of the cupboard where I'd been hiding, and one to the classroom door. He'd warned the hostages that these devices were linked to the others around the room. Any attempt to leave by either door would trigger them all. And so he kept them terrified, silent and immobile, while he was pursuing me.

I learned all this and more from Mum and Bree, when they visited me in hospital. Well, mostly from Bree. Mum was in too much of a state to say very much. She sat by my bed, sobbing quietly, and we held hands or she would stroke my hair.

I am less anxious about Mum now. Although I dislike Dr Macdonald, I trust her and I know that Mum will get the help she needs.

Bree has been told by the doctors not to upset me, so even though I can sense that she's *dying* to ask me why I stayed behind in school that day, she hasn't.

But she has filled in all the gaps for me and told me everything. How the explosive device that Lee was still carrying in his rucksack was actually the *only* one he made up correctly. Apparently the ones he left in the classroom were duds and wouldn't have gone off in a million years – as Bree says, Lee always *was* in the lowest set for science. When he threw his rucksack off, he detonated the device. Then the police stormed the building and the siege was over. Lee was seriously injured, but he'll recover, eventually.

Bree also brought in a whole heap of newspapers, both local and national. Everyone is calling me a heroine.

I'm sure Kat Randall is *very* grateful to me.

Is it really only a few weeks since she stopped me at the school gates and grabbed my tie and almost choked me? It seems a million years ago, in a different universe.

After everything that has happened, I know I will never be scared of Kat Randall again. And as I told Lee Curtis, I won't be bullied by anyone else, *ever*.

Not even by Dr Macdonald.

* * *

I go into our next session, all guns blazing (ha ha), and begin by staring challengingly at Dr Macdonald.

'You haven't asked me yet what I am sure you're absolutely *dying* to know,' I say. 'That's not meant to be funny, by the way.'

Dr Macdonald refuses to rise to the bait. 'If there's something you want to tell me, Mia, go ahead,' she replies calmly.

'You want to know why, if Jamie is a ghost, I believed so strongly that he could hold thirty-three people hostage,' I state confidently. 'So strongly, in fact, that I put my own life in danger to stop him.'

Dr Macdonald says nothing, she just looks at me. I feel a terrible urge to throw a cushion at her.

'What you have to understand, first of all, is that Jamie was trying to help me.' I am impatient and I speak quickly, words tumbling out. 'Everything that happened, all the bad things he did, all the times he tried to make me stand up to Mum and get her help, were for *me*. He tried to give me courage. He tried to make me brave so that I wouldn't go through life being walked all over. He wanted to give me the kind of future that he would never have, that he would never have the chance to experience. And besides . . .' I can't help giving Dr Macdonald a triumphant glance. 'I know for certain that Jamie is a ghost and that he isn't just inside my head. He is separate to, and outside of me. I know, *because other people have seen him.*'

Dr Macdonald does not look either impressed or underwhelmed. She simply *looks.*

'I see,' she says. 'So Jamie can appear to other people, but he doesn't do it on a regular basis, I take it. Why do you think that is, Mia?'

'Oh, God, I don't know all the rules of the spirit world, do I?' I mutter irritably. 'The point is that other people have seen him too. Not just me.'

Dr Macdonald does not react. For pity's sake, I've already told her my story from start to finish. Surely she remembers?

'Just to remind you,' I add with a hint of sarcasm, 'I *know* that Grandpa saw Jamie too.'

'You mean when he was ill?' Dr Macdonald asks. She says nothing more, but we both know she is referring indirectly to the fact that Grandpa was drugged and dazed for the last few weeks of his life.

'He could see Jamie the day he died,' I assert stubbornly. 'I know he could.'

Dr Macdonald and I are fencing with each other. I say what I know to be true, however far-fetched it may seem, and she challenges me, without really seeming to, with cold, hard logic.

'I also told you about Doctor Zeelander,' I say, looking her straight in the eye. Imagine the old Mia Jackson having the nerve to do that. 'When she refused to talk to us about Mum, Jamie got so angry, he smashed the in-tray off the desk. Doctor Zeelander could *see* him then. I could tell by her face. She was petrified.'

Dr Macdonald nods thoughtfully. 'Did she say anything at the time?'

'No, but we can ask her,' I say defiantly. 'Or maybe you think Doctor Zeelander was seeing things too.'

'Certainly we could ask her,' Dr Macdonald agrees, much to my surprise.

'And then there's Mum,' I sweep on, determined

to convince her. 'She hasn't seen Jamie, but from what she says I think she can hear us talking sometimes—'

'Mia, your mum suffers from bi-polar disorder – also known as manic depression,' Dr Macdonald says quietly. 'Hallucinations, both visual and auditory, can be a feature of the condition.'

'Maybe you think *I've* inherited Mum's illness,' I snap back. I'm joking, but Dr Macdonald does not smile.

'Look.' My nervous energy takes over and I jump to my feet and begin to pace the room. 'I know you don't believe that Jamie is a ghost. I know you think I've made this up. But other people have seen him, not just me. Maybe he didn't do those things I told you about, but it seems too much of a coincidence, doesn't it? And if Jamie didn't do them, who did? There's no one else . . .'

Dr Macdonald says nothing. The light is fading outside and she switches on her desk lamp. All the while she regards me steadily but does not speak.

Realization hits me like a punch to the head. My

knees are suddenly no longer able to bear my weight and I sink down onto my chair.

'*You think it was me*,' I summon up the strength to whisper. '*You think I'm Jamie.*'

'I did not say that, Mia,' Dr Macdonald replies. For the first time I hear a hint of compassion in her voice. '*You're* saying it.'

'But—'

Confused, I press my fingers to my temples. They are burning and yet my hands are ice-cold. 'You think that I'm two people inside my own head? That's not possible! I *talk* to Jamie. I *touch* him. I *see* him!'

My voice cracks with shock. I have always thought of Jamie and myself as two halves of one whole. Now it seems we could be even more closely entwined than that.

A split personality.

Two people in just one mind and one body.

Mine.

I don't believe it. I *won't* believe it. But over the course of our sessions, Dr Macdonald's slow yet effective *drip-drip-drip* technique has silently been wearing away at what I thought I knew, like acid eating away metal.

'If I'd done all that stuff, I would remember, wouldn't I?' I blurt out. My mind seems to have fractured into tiny pieces that are flying off in all directions, and I can't seem to hold one thought long enough to examine it before I'm racing on to the next. 'I'd remember setting fire to my father's house, I'd remember breaking Michael Riley's arm, I'd remember wrecking Doctor Zeelander's car and all the rest of it?'

'Not necessarily, Mia,' Dr Macdonald replies evenly. 'The mind has a way of playing tricks on us. It has fantastic abilities to fool us and make us think that black is white and vice versa.'

'But I *saw* Jamie going to the annexe before the siege,' I burst out. There are *so* many reasons why this cannot be true, and why I don't want it to be true. But Dr Macdonald's calm, controlled logic has crept up and caught me unawares in its stifling, vice-like grip.

'So you said,' she replies. 'And then what happened?'

'I thought Jamie was going to do something drastic

243

to make Mum realize we'd had enough,' I reply slowly. 'I didn't know *what*, but I thought he might target Kat Randall because she was bullying me. So I went out of our classroom because—'

I stop for a second. I feel so confused, but I try to go on. 'I was going to the annexe because . . .'

My voice falters again.

It wasn't Jamie who was going to the annexe to take revenge on Kat Randall in some way that would get everyone's attention, including Mum's. It wasn't Jamie who couldn't go ahead, in the end, because Lee Curtis had had other plans.

It was me.

I can't remember what I had in mind, what I was planning to do.

But it was me.

I am shaking. I curl myself into a tight ball, hugging my knees, my hair falling over my face.

'Am I very ill?' I ask haltingly.

Dr Macdonald is speaking and the tone of her voice is reassuring, but I'm not listening to what she is saying. I am replaying the last fourteen years in my head.

Ms Kennedy has always told me that I have a wonderful imagination, a writer's imagination, but now it has been my downfall.

I look back into the past and wonder wildly if it is possible that 'Jamie', reckless, wild, quick-tempered, is the other side of meek and mild little Mia. Have I always had that other personality inside me?

It would explain how I found the courage and the nerve to fight my way into the annexe and outwit Lee Curtis. The intense rage I felt when Ms Kennedy tried to make me leave the school and when Leo Jackson and Dr Zeelander refused to help us; that anger was mine and it was Jamie's. It was Jamie's idea to force Mum to get help by whatever means possible, but it was mine too.

I am Mia.

I am Jamie.

I'm lying in my hospital bed, out of sight under the blankets, and I am crying.

I cannot hold back the tears for the brother I thought I knew, but who only existed in my head and nowhere else. The brother I used ruthlessly to show the rage and loathing and fear that mouse-like Mia did not dare to express. Could all those explosive feelings have been hidden deep inside me for so many years without me realizing?

It appears that I *am* very ill, even more sick than Mum.

'I'm sorry, Jamie,' I murmur.

But what's the point?

I am only apologizing to myself.

Night is falling and the nurse has not come in yet to draw the blinds. My little room is dimly lit by the lamp that stands on my locker and the air is scented with the freesias Mum brought today. She is subdued and still very anxious about me. But her anxiety has made her determined to seek help, and Dr Macdonald has already set the wheels in motion.

An astounding thing happened today. Mum told me that Leo Jackson had been in touch. What a shock. Mum looked immensely awkward and embarrassed, and it took her at least five minutes to get the words out. I did not tell her that I have already met him, and I don't think Leo has told her either. I shall tell Mum later, though.

No more secrets.

Leo has seen the newspapers and is now offering to pay Mum child support. Guilty conscience? Who knows? I wonder if he'll backdate it fourteen years. But, anyway, it will be a big help.

I did not ask Mum if Leo wants to have any kind of relationship with me. I shall find that out later, though, and it will only happen if I want it to, and it will be on my terms.

Bree can't wait for me to come back to school. There's to be some sort of ceremony and I'll be awarded a medal for my bravery during the siege. I shall apologize to Ms Kennedy and ask for her help in planning my future career as a writer.

There's so much to look forward to when I am finally well.

I curl my knees tightly towards me so that I'm in the foetal position, a baby in the comforting, womb-like warmth of the bed. Then I wipe away the tears with the back of my hand; I know for sure that I am stronger now, just as Jamie wanted.

'Goodbye, Jamie,' I murmur softly as hope for the future floods through me and my heart lifts. 'I don't need you any more.'

About the author

Narinder was born and brought up in Wolverhampton, with two younger sisters. She studied English at Birmingham University and then worked as a primary school teacher, but always loved writing. After winning several short story prizes, she was encouraged to take the leap and devote herself to writing. Her very first book was accepted by a publisher and she's now been a full-time author for several years.

To relax, Narinder loves reading murder mysteries and watching football (she supports Wolves); she also loves travelling and is learning Italian. She lives with her husband and their three cats in Cambridge. For more information, visit **www.narinderdhami**.com.

OStRICH BOYs

by KEITH GRAY

Shortlisted for the Costa Children's Book Award

'It's not really kidnapping, is it? He'd have to be alive for it to be proper kidnapping.'

Kenny, Sim and Blake are grieving for their best friend Ross and angered by his inadequate memorial service. So they steal his ashes and set out to take Ross to Ross – a tiny hamlet in Scotland – to give him the send-off his family failed to provide.

Driven by black comedy and packing a massive punch, *Ostrich Boys* takes readers on an unmissable road trip.

'I loved it . . . a wonderful book' *Jacqueline Wilson*

'Reminiscent of *On the Road* and *Catcher in the Rye* . . . a profound work, instantly worthy of the label "modern classic"' *Bookseller*

'A remarkable book!' *Carousel*

'Funny, page-turning and profound'
The Sunday Times

ISBN: 978 0 099 45657 5